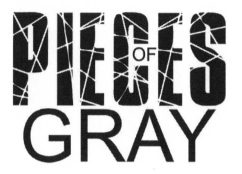

PIECES OF GRAY

Kelly Moore

Broken Pieces Series in order

Broken Pieces

Pieced Together

Piece by Piece, Steel's Rescue

Pieces of Gray

Syn's Broken Journey, releases 2017

Other books

Next August

This August coming 2017

Edited by Tami Rogers - Queen Editing

Cover Design – Kennedy Kelly Cover Crush Designs

Paperback Formatting – Brenda Wright – Formatting Done Wright

Follow me at:

www.kellymooreauthor.com and sign up for my Newsletter to get exclusives

Join my review/street group on Facebook at Moore Romance Group

Follow me on fb at http://on.fb.me/1P9G9V4

Amazon http://amzn.to/1mU6Y9p

Goodreads http://bit.ly/1RkemHh

Cover design by Kennedy Kelly at Cover Crush Designs

This is a work of fiction. Names, characters, places and incidents are either the product of the author's imagination or are used fictitiously, and any resemblance to actual persons, living or dead, business establishments, events or locals is entirely coincidental

Table of Contents

CHAPTER

"low down, Gray! Where the hell do you think you're going?" He grabs me by my arm.

"What are you doing here, Syn? You need to stay out of this," I snap at him and then I wrench my arm away from him. My backpack slides off my shoulder and falls to the ground making me stumble. I'm able to catch myself, but it only adds to my annoyance that he followed me.

"You left the wedding like your feet were on fire." He picks up my bag and hands it to me. "You can't just disappear and not say anything to anyone. You're stupid if you thought for one second that I wouldn't hunt you down," he bites out.

"This doesn't concern you!" I yank my bag from him.

"Come on, Gray. It's me we're talking about here. You know I can't watch you leave for trouble. And you're wrong, you're my family, whatever concerns you directly affects me." His brows are drawn together.

I pull him to the side out of earshot. "I have to help, but Captain Maynard will not let me join the rescue team. He says that I'm too close to the situation," I growl. "I refuse to sit back and

1

not help the man I love." I swallow hard. "If there's a chance he's still alive." I'm fighting back so many emotions.

"**Last call for Flight 410 to China**!" blares over the intercom.

"Please..." I beg him, "Let me go!" People are starting to stare at us. I don't want a big scene. Or a fight.

"No. Not like this." He grabs me by the arm again and leads me to an exit.

It's everything I can do just to refrain from letting the tears flow. I want to scream out to get someone's attention. Of course, airport security would come running, but I know deep down he wants to help.

He drags me through the long galleys without another word. Then he opens the door to his Jeep and places me inside like a broken child. I watch him as he throws my bag in the back and climbs behind the wheel, the leather seat creaks as he climbs in behind it.

I have half a mind to jump out and run back inside, but I know he would only follow me again anyway. "You won't be doing this alone," he growls and then peels out of the parking garage.

"I've already told you that Captain Maynard will not let me go. I have to do this on my own!" I yell at him.

He ignores me and continues racing in and out of highway traffic causing me to buckle up and hold on for my life.

Years of guilt and anguish are running through my mind, twisting any possibility of clear thinking about this situation.

His face is burned into my soul. I've never forgotten him or even how loved he made me feel. I lost him once. If there is any chance at all that he's still alive, I have to get to him. Right now the stubborn man behind the wheel is in my way.

"Syn! Stop the car!" I yell out in emotional torment.

He abruptly swerves through two lanes of traffic squealing to a dead stop on the side of the road creating a hue of dust around us.

"You have to listen to me... Crew could be alive and I have to help him."

"I heard what you said, but I'm not letting you go rogue to find him. I'll take the mission and take you with me. What did you think you were going to do once you got to China? You know they're still arresting Americans over there for the least little thing and an angry brunette would only draw suspicion. You have no weapons and no way of protecting yourself." He sits facing me.

"I would've had plenty of time on the plane for planning. I still have some contacts in the field that I could've used to get my hands on a rifle. You know perfectly well that I'm more than capable of taking care of myself," I spit out.

"That's not good enough!" He pauses to regain his composure. "You know you're too close to this. That's exactly why the captain told you to sit back and let someone else do the work. Let me help you, Gray." He touches my hand.

He's always had my back. He and Steel are brothers and they're my cousins, but they've always treated me like a sister. We have built such a strong bond between us especially after rescuing Steel's new bride, Adyson. I should feel bad about rushing out of their wedding, but the mere mention of Kell Crew sent me into a tailspin.

It has been two years since I was rescued from that hell hole of torture. The Chinese held us in small cages deep in the jungle. I was told Crew was dead from a drowning torture, but I still searched for him before the Army soldiers rescued twenty of us. Tears finally fall at the thought that he has suffered for another two years.

"Look, I know what Captain Maynard said. But he doesn't have the final word. His clout is with the Air Force, you're forgetting that you and I are in the Army. We answer to someone else." He grins.

"General Scott..." I breathe out with new excitement.

"That's right, sweetheart. I've already linked up with him. And by the way, don't ever ignore my synch again. I'll just keep screaming in your head until you answer me." His face looks softer.

"I'm sorry, sometimes I hate our mic implants. I just didn't want to put you in any more danger, and I definitely don't want Steel giving up his honeymoon to help me out." I wipe at the last tear right before it rolls down my cheek.

"Steel will not miss his honeymoon with Ady. You and I are going to do this together, but we are going to do it with the support of the Army behind us. I know you are willing to risk your life for him. But I'm not willing to sit back and watch that happen, not when I can help."

"Okay, we'll try it your way. But if it doesn't work, I'm going on my own."

Syn eases back out into traffic, but it doesn't take long before he is driving like a bat out of hell again.

I'm so thankful that Steel didn't get his link fixed, he would still be screaming at me to answer him right now. He didn't want anyone to be able to interrupt him on his honeymoon to New Zealand. I'm glad that he and Ady found one another again. The two of them have conquered so many obstacles to be together. Steel has finally come to grips with losing his leg and Ady came too close to death. They deserve to be happy.

It gives me hope that if Crew is still alive that he and I can be together. My fear is that he won't be the same man I fell in love with. I know it took me some time to readjust and I closed my feelings off. Syn is the first person that I confided in. I need to trust him. My parents don't even know all the dirty details of my capture and torture. I keep my scars concealed well, both the outward and inward ones.

"Where are we going?" I ask him.

"Back to Steel's fortress for supplies."

"If we go back there, then he's going to want to come with us."

4

"I promise that is not going to happen. If he wants to help, then he can help where he stands. He can set us up with the right pilot to get us in the remote area that we need. We're not going to just be able to fly into China by commercial airlines and get everyone out. Their military will have us all strung up."

I know he's right. If we don't do this right, we could all be held captive. I wouldn't survive that again.

My dad and Uncle Kyren are cleaning up as we pull onto Steel's property. Captain Maynard meets us at the Jeep before we can even get out.

"I received a link from General Scott. I guess I don't have a choice but to help you. I wish you would've just let this play out with our men in place." He looks a little angry.

"If Crew was a member of your team, you would be the first person out of here to help him," I add.

He throws his hands up in surrender. "Let me help you get a plan together."

"I could use the groom," Syn says.

Kyren and my dad walk up. "Are you okay, angel? Captain Maynard filled us in on what's going on."

"I'm okay, Dad. I just really want to get over there to help out." He hugs me to him.

"I don't like the idea of you going back over to China. It scares the hell out of me."

"I know Dad, but someone I love may still be there and I have to help him. It's not any different than any other mission I've been on. No mission is safe, there's always a risk. This time, it involves someone that I love."

He lets go of me. "Steel left strict instructions to interrupt him if Syn was able to stop you and bring you back."

"He's had what? A good ten minutes alone with Ady. That should be all he needs." Syn says laughing.

5

"There is something that is just not right about you, Syn." I playfully slap the back of his head.

"What?" he asks, still laughing.

I shake my head at him. "You're an idiot."

"While this idiot interrupts only God knows what, you need to go to Steel's armory and get weapons and ammo together. Maybe grab some snacks while you're in there." He points in the direction.

Captain Maynard, Kyren, and Dad, all help me load duffel bags with everything we're going to need. Syn appears in the doorway with Steel, who is pulling his shirt over his head.

He opens his arms and I freely walk into them. "I'm so sorry to mess up your honeymoon night."

"Ady and I have forever together, don't you worry about it. Besides, you put your life on the line to help rescue Ady, she wouldn't have it any other way and neither would I."

"I don't know what you're complaining about, you already had your ten minutes alone with her. You were probably already done and Ady is sound asleep." Syn says snorting with laughter.

All of us yell "Asshole!" at him in perfect unison and Steel gives him an obscene hand gesture.

"Gray, let's go up to my office. I need to make some quick connections, via my computer link, so I can see what is the earliest we can get you in the air. My brother will be a little delayed because I'm going to kick his ass." He points at Syn.

"Ah, funny man. I'm sure you just used up all your energy during your ten minutes." Syn laughs again.

Kyren steps between his sons. "Go get your cousin set up. I'll take care of your little brother." He puts the emphasis on the word 'little' and we all burst out laughing.

"You guys are so not funny," Syn says, but laughs as he says it.

For the next hour, I listen to Steel juggle multiple things to put it all together. Syn and I have a flight on a military plane that will be leaving at six in the morning. He managed to convince the Portland airport to let the military pilot land there to pick us up.

Steel hands me a piece of paper with detailed instructions on it for the pilot. He also lets us know who to contact when we are ready for extraction.

"I'm sorry all this happened on your wedding day. Please tell Ady that I said so," I apologize.

"Think nothing of it. You'd do the same for any of us and she knows it. I'm getting my link fixed in the morning before we fly to New Zealand, so you make sure you let me know if there is anything else I can do for you. Be safe and if you find Crew, bring him home." He hugs me again. "I'd love to meet the man that stole your heart."

"You go back to Ady, we got the rest of this covered. Thank you." I walk back downstairs and every single light is on. My mom, Cady, and my aunt, Brogan, have joined the rest of the gang looking over Syn's shoulder.

"What's going on down here?" I ask. Mom runs over and hugs me.

"I hope you find him, Baby. Please promise me that you'll be safe." She sniffs.

"I will, Mom."

"Come over here and review the map with Syn," Captain Maynard orders.Syn has the best navigational skills that I've ever seen. He may be a jokester and a two-year-old most of the time, but he's also very smart and highly skilled. He has somehow managed to print out the jungle landscape where I was once held captive. He points to an area due west of my former prison.

"Here... this is where a team scouting came upon five of our men held in cages similar to what you described. Two of the men said there were two more soldiers being held underground, but they've been unable to pinpoint the location to gain entry. The last word we received from any of them is that they were surrounded by the Chinese army. Another team has been deployed to help them out."

I reach over Syn's shoulder and grab his laser pointer, it has a red light that measures distance. I trace the line between where I was held captive and where they were being held. "It's only a little over a mile from where I was held as a prisoner. We checked the areas around us but didn't find anything. He was that close!" A sob comes out. "We left them behind. I left Crew behind!"

Syn stands up. "You did the best you could to get out of there alive and you don't know if Crew is even still alive or not, so don't start feeling guilty about something that was out of your hands. You were a prisoner, just like him," he reminds me sternly.

"You're right. I need to stay focused on our mission so that we can rescue all of these men." He nods his head at me and sits back down. I feel my dad's hand grip my shoulder for support.

"There's something else I found…" He points to another area on the map.

"Looking at the geography, this area here… is the only place where an underground prison could be built."

Captain Maynard leans in for a closer look. "He's right. I'll link with General Scott and let him know."

"Before you make that call, don't let him send a team in until we get the other soldiers out alive," Syn implores.

Captain Maynard nods his head and leaves the room to get in contact with the general on his link.

"It's already after midnight. Why don't we all go get a little sleep before you take off? Cady and I will go pack up some food and some supplies for you to take with you," Aunt Brogan says.

"That's a good idea. Gray, you and I need to discuss details of our plan in the airplane."

I tell each of them good night and one by one they all disperse, except my dad is lingering.

"I'll come home safely, I promise." I hug him this time.

"If I thought I could be helpful to you, I'd be on that plane with you in the morning. You've trained for this. I feel useless to you." He sounds sad.

I pull back from him. "Don't ever say that. You've been my biggest supporter. I know you didn't want me to join the army, but you supported it. You taught me how to shoot and defend myself. When I came back home, you never pushed me. You let me work it out in my own time. I knew you were always there if I needed you, so in some way, you go with me on every mission. I love you, Dad."

He hugs me harder. "I love you, angel.

We unfold from our embrace. "While you're over there, could you make sure Syn doesn't get himself killed by pissing the off wrong people?"

I laugh at him. "I'll do my best to keep him out of trouble, but I'm not promising anything. He's a wild card. You never know, I just may shoot him myself."

"That would not surprise me, but then you would have my sister to deal with. I wouldn't wish that on anyone." He laughs

"Where do you think Syn gets it from? I love Aunt Brogan to death, but I wouldn't want to piss her off, even if I am a skilled marksman. I think she could take us all out if we messed with either of her children."

"I knew I raised a smart woman." He laughs again.

"Goodnight, Dad."

"Night, angel."

CHAPTER

I wish Steel could've arranged some way for us to bypass security. Since the war started several years ago, flights have been almost eliminated overseas, but security is massive, even for military personnel. The process is long and daunting. You feel violated by the time the search is over.

Syn bounces through the security gate with a smile.

"I don't know what you have to smile about, that was awful. I almost thought they were going to perform a cavity search." I scowl at him.

"I got the cute brunettes link name," he announces proudly, as he shoves a piece of paper in his pocket.

"Only you could get a strip search and come out with a girl's link." I can't help but laugh at him. He's such a player. I don't think anyone will ever get that big heart of his, only his body. I'm a one woman man, and that man for me has always been Kell Crew.

We finally board the plane for our long flight. Steel did well. He got us on a private military plane, meaning it's very comfortable and well stocked. Syn heads straight for the co-pilot seat and I pick a comfy spot and recline my seat back. My mind immediately drifts to the first time I met the attractive badass Captain Kell Crew...

Pieces of Gray

I'd been reassigned platoons. Crews unit had recently lost their best sniper, and I was to be his replacement. It was bone melting hot outside and the tents didn't provide any relief. I was directed to Captain Crew's tent as soon as I got there. The guard at the tent asked me my name and when I told him, he looked a bit confused but allowed me to go inside through the flap in the tent. When I walked in, this hulk of a man had his back to me and was changing out of his t-shirt. My mouth watered at the sight of the muscles rippling down his back as he raised his arms over his head. A moan must have escaped my lips because he turned toward me.

"Who are you?" He barked. "I think you must be in the wrong tent."

"I'm Lieutenant Gray Milby, Sir. I'm the sniper you requested."

"You're a woman," he growled.

"Yes, Sir! I am told that a lot. The last time I checked, yes I was. Thank you, Sir." That's when the most beautiful thing happened.

He smiled.

The minute he did it, my heart melted. He stood six foot five to my five-ten frame. His hair color matched my deep chocolate color and his eyes were a deeper shade of brown than mine. My eyes have specks of green, but his were all a creamy chocolate brown. Clean shaven, but I could see an early hint of a dark shadow on his face. I imagined that he would have been sexy as hell with a beard. My insides fluttered. I was a twenty-one-year-old virgin standing in front of this hunk of a man that I should've been totally intimated by, but instead, I felt the thumping of my heart for the first time ever.

"Gray, I hear that you're the best sniper in the Army. Come show me what you got, Lieutenant." I would've followed him anywhere he led me. He walked me to the range where other snipers were already practicing.

He opened a container full of different types of military rifles. "Pick your beast, Gray."

I took off my duffel bag. "I have my own, Sir." I pulled out my rifle and handed it to him to inspect.

"Nice. Is this military approved?" He looked through the scope.

"Yes, Sir. It's an Accuracy International L11543. All the extras have been approved."

He handed it back to me. "The range is all yours. May I suggest you start with the closest target?" He stood tall and larger than life, behind me.

I smirked at him before I laid down and took aim at the furthest target out in the field. I focused my scope and anchored my elbow in the dirt.

Breathe in, breathe out. On my breath out, I pulled the trigger and waited.

I heard a whistle come from the soldier holding the binoculars. "Captain, Sir, that's a clean hit at 2,600 yards." The soldier looked at me and smiled.

"Gray, where did you learn how to shoot like that?"

"I grew up with a bunch of macho cousins and a dad who knew a thing or two about rifles."

He walked up to me and looked down as I got off the ground. "Damn good shot, for a woman." He smirked.

I don't know what possessed me to say it, but I couldn't help myself, "I think it was a damn good shot for anyone, Crew." I gritted out, as my eyes blazed into his.

I'd never been disrespectful to anyone in the military before, but this man felt comfortable enough to call me by my name rather than my rank.

He was under my skin, but not in a bad way. I wasn't brave enough to call him by his first name, so Crew was what came out. I waited for his wrath, but instead I got his laughter. I was a goner after that.

12

"Earth to Gray." Syn is kneeling in front of me. "Hey, you okay? I've been calling your name for a while now."

"Yeah, I'm fine. I was just thinking about the first time I met Crew." I smile at him.

"When we land it's going to be daylight in China. You may want to try to get ahead of the time difference by napping as much as possible."

"I'm not sure if I can sleep. I tossed and turned for the little amount of time we had last night."

He hands me some earphones. "Why don't you try a movie? That always seems to bore you to death." He laughs.

"Thanks for making this all happen."

"Don't thank me yet, Sweetheart. We got a long way to go." He returns to the cockpit.

My thoughts drift again.

He stalked into my tent. There was no other way to describe it. Our day had been miserably long and hot in the field. I took out two Chinese soldiers to save two of our men, but we lost one. Crew took every loss personally. We didn't make it back into camp until after midnight. Exhaustion had overtaken me and I was in desperate need of a shower. Being the only woman in our platoon, the guys had built a shower for me inside my tent. I stripped and the layers of dust suspended in the air. The shower never stayed hot for too long, so I washed quickly. Just as I was rinsing my hair, I heard my name. I blinked the water from my eyes and there he stood staring at me from the doorway.

"What is it, Crew?" His look was consuming. He walked over and grabbed a towel and held it out for me.

I hesitantly took it from him. I was a young innocent girl, but I recognized the look in his eyes because my eyes burned with the same hot desire.

I told myself that I was brave with every aspect of my life and there was no way I would back out of this now, nor did I even want to. I took the towel from his hand purposely touching him. His inhale was sharp at the contact which fed my boldness. I lightly dried my hair and then stepped out in front of him completely naked. His eyes followed the towel as it fell to the floor and then they climbed my body an inch at a time. I heard his deep sexy moan. It made me squeeze my thighs together to dull the ache that sound created.

"You're a very beautiful woman," he growled as he stepped closer.

I matched his step. "And you have too many damn clothes on." If I was going to be brave, then I was going all the way. I had no idea what I was doing, I only knew how he made my body feel.

He ripped his t-shirt off and my mouth watered.A fierce ache started between my legs at the sight of his bare chest. He sat down on my bed and removed his dusty boots. He unbuckled his pants and removed them along with his boxers, all while his eyes remained glued to mine. That ache grew stronger into a desperate need like I had never felt before.

"Do you mind if I use your shower?" He strutted by me and my eyes followed his fine muscular ass. My curiosity got the better of me and I stood where I could see him showering.

I knew the water was cold and I'd always heard that cold water causes shrinkage in a man. If he has shrunk, then I'm in big trouble. His cock would never fit inside of me.

He grabbed the towel off the floor and wiped the droplets off that were running down his chest to his goody trail. I licked my lips wishing that I could lap the droplets up with my tongue.He closed the distance between us. "You're one incredible woman."

He kissed me softly at first, I eagerly opened up to him and our tongues mingled and his kiss became more possessive. He was owning me with his mouth and my body yielded to him. I felt myself soften.

"You taste so damn sweet," he moaned into my mouth. His hands roughly found my ass.

"Crew, I have to tell you something before we go any further," I whispered to him.

"Don't tell me you have a boyfriend back home, because as far as I'm concerned, you will never want to be with him again when I'm done fucking you." He hiked my leg over his hip.

I gasped at the feel of me wrapped around him. "That's just it. I have never been with a man," I whispered into his neck.

He pulled back slightly to look into my eyes. "You mean no other man has ever touched you?" he asked, gently.

"No man has ever touched me," I shyly admitted.

He growled into my mouth and continued kissing me. He released my leg and walked me backward onto the bed.

"This doesn't change what's about to happen between us, does it?" I asked, hoping to God he would say no.

"The only thing it changes is how rough I can be. I was planning on just fucking you. Now I will take my time and worship every glorious inch of you to bring you nothing but pleasure for your first time. You'll never need or want another man."

He was right. He did everything he promised multiple times and ruined me for any other man. I've been completely alone since I lost him. We had to keep our relationship very discreet or I'd risk being reassigned to another unit. I think the sneaking around made our relationship even sexier.

We came up with a safe word. We would use the word, *canoodle,* in a sentence if we wanted to escape alone if other soldiers were around us. It got quite funny hearing Crew try to make a sentence with canoodle in it, without sounding like a complete pansy.

One day he just yelled "Canoodle!" and everyone in the room turned and looked at him. He simply said, "I'm sorry," and left the room. I met up with him in his barracks and he jumped me the minute I walked inside.

"We have to change our safe word." He covered his mouth with mine to stop me from laughing. "How about I just say, 'I'm horny'? That would be much easier to work into a sentence and nobody would think anything of it."

I hear Steel's link sync in my ear. "Gray, can you hear me?"

"Loud and clear. Why are you calling me from your honeymoon?"

"I'm not, I'm on the plane to New Zealand. Ady was worried about you, so she insisted that I talk to you before we landed."

"I'm in good hands. Thanks for the nice lift. The plane is very comfortable. I'm anxious to get my feet on the ground and start searching for Crew."

"Honey, you know there's a good chance that he isn't alive," he reminds me with concern.

"I know, but I'll never forgive myself if I don't look for him. He would've never left me out there." I speak the last part in a whimper.

"You thought he was dead. You were half dead yourself, according to Syn. If you thought he was alive for one minute, we would've been carrying your body out of there because you would've died looking for him."

"After I was told he was dead, I didn't believe it because I didn't feel it. I thought it was my mind playing tricks on me because I didn't want him to be dead. I shoved those feelings down deep in order to survive without him, that feeling finally faded over time, but now they're back. I feel him. It's like he is calling to me."

"I believe you. I understand that you feel like part of you died along with him. You've always been one of the sweetest, smartest, and most determined women that I know. When you're not in uniform that is, because then you're a complete badass."

I laugh at his description of me. "Thanks for believing in me. It really means a lot coming from you. Now get back to your honeymoon before I tell Syn you're linked with me. You know he will make some degrading remark to you about sex."

He laughs. "I'm out."

I finally doze off for a few hours, but I suddenly wake due to the bouncing of the plane. "Hey, what are you guys doing up there?" I yell through my link.

"Sorry, we're flying into a storm. If we go around it, our landing will be delayed for a couple of hours and we already have soldiers waiting for us to land. Stay buckled," Syn adds.

I try the earphones to drown out my thoughts. No such luck. My mind goes to a time that Crew thought I was dead.

We were on a mission to save an American family that was unable to get out of China when they mandated it. One of their kids was sick and not allowed to fly. The Chinese government tried to force them to leave the child behind. They were fortunate enough to escape from them and hide in a hut, deep in the jungle. The couple was able to get word to the American government as to their exact location. It should've been a routine mission.

The Chinese learned of their location also and sent forces out to kill them. Our troop fought them off while I found a high enough place to lower down and take them out one by one.

I heard a noise and took my eyes from my scope and a grenade rolled by me. I quickly rolled off the ledge I had climbed on before it exploded.

I barely heard Crew screaming my name. My ears were ringing. I was choked on the dust and smoke and was dazed from the blow to my head. While coughing and struggling to breathe, I couldn't find my voice to answer him. I had to get out of the path of the fire, my escape took me even further down the hill and away from my unit.

It took me a few minutes to regain my composure before I could locate a way to avoid the flames and return. As I came up behind my team, I saw Crew on his knees with his head hanging down. I called his name, but he didn't hear me. I called his name again and touched his shoulder. He jumped off the ground and held me to him. It was the first time he had shown any affection toward me in front of his men.

"I thought I'd lost you." He had tears and dirt running down his face. "Don't ever scare me like that again." He kissed me softly. "I love you."

It was the first time I heard these words pass his lips and I knew I felt them for him, too. "I love you, too," I rasped out. The next thing that happened completely surprised me. Every soldier in our troop encompassed the two of us in a hug, one big sweaty, smelly group hug. I loved it.

We rescued the family and brought them safely back to America. After we got back to our camp, Crew made sure he told me he loved me every time he saw me.

That night, I snuck into his barracks. I wanted to taste him for the first time. He always controlled me during sex. Not that I was complaining, but I wanted to know what it felt like to give him complete pleasure.

I stole two pairs of handcuffs from his desk drawer and quietly locked them around his wrists before I attached them to his bed. I climbed on top of him and kissed his chin causing him to wake up immediately and yank against his restraints.

"What's this?" He smiled.

"I want to play." I offered him a flirtatious smile.

"All you had to do was ask. I'll gladly play with you."

"I wanted to freely play with you." I sat up and ran my hands down his chest until I reached the band of his pants when I heard his cuffs clink.

"You can take these off." He smiled.

"I will if you're AFRAID." My hand grasped his hard cock.

"I'm not afraid," he gritted out.

"I didn't think so. Sit back and enjoy." I hoped he would enjoy it. I'd never had a man in my mouth before. I leaned down and licked the tip placing just the head in my mouth and swirled it around. He moaned.I took that as a good sign and proceeded to put him further in my mouth. I sucked hard and I heard him gasp out.

"Teeth, baby, teeth!" he chanted shrilly. "Watch the teeth!"

I covered my teeth with my lips and started over. His moans became louder. Placing my hand on the lower part of his shaft, I stroked him up and down as I continued the same action with my mouth.

"Baby, if you don't stop that, I'm going to come in your pretty little mouth. So unless you're ready for that, I suggest you stop now."

I wetly popped him out of my mouth. "I want all of you." I continued stroking him and swallowing him as far as I could go. He let out a roar and exploded into my mouth. I licked him until he stopped pulsating. I climbed up along his body and unlocked his cuffs. Leaning over him, I let my breasts drag along his chest as I rubbed my body against him. I kissed his lips so that he could taste himself on me.

"Goodnight," I said softly.

"Wait, you're not staying?"

Climbing off of him I answer, "Nope. I'd never done that before and I wanted to see if I was any good at it." I looked at his limp cock. "I guess I did a good job."

He woke me up the next night with his mouth between my legs. He taught me what he liked and let me experiment without judgment. He knew my body and what brought me pleasure more than I did. He was very skilled in the love making department.

I never asked him how he got so talented in bed. He was seven years older than me and I'm sure I wasn't his first sexual partner, but I knew I wanted to be his last.

It wasn't just the sex with him, though.

The only personal item I carried with me, was a copy of *Jane Eyre* by Charlotte Bronte that my mother gave to me. She would read it to me every night and I found comfort in it amongst all the dangers that I faced in the war. The pages were yellowed and bent from so much use.

Crew found me curled up late one night under the covers using my flashlight to read. He scared me to death when he yanked back the blankets.

"What are you doing under there?" he laughed.

"I wanted to read and not wake you up."

He sat up in the middle of the bed and drew me into his lap. "Read to me, baby."

"It's not exactly a manly book," I stated shyly.

"I don't care if it is or not. I want to be part of whatever you're doing. If that means listening to some sappy romance, then I'm all in." He drew me closer. "If you want to read me an erotic story, then I'll gladly roll play with you." He nipped my ear.

I told him about my mother reading this book to me over and over again when I was a little girl. After that night, I would come in to find Crew with *Jane Eyre* in his lap, ready to read to me. He truly loved spending time with me.

When we were captured, the Chinese soldiers ransacked our bags. I watched as they threw my only possession into a fire pit and the pages curled into a black pile of nothing.

The plane jars me again. Syn's voice is in my ear. "Hold on tight, Gray. We're going to have to make an emergency landing. One of our engines took a hit by lightning." I set my chair upright and pull my buckle tighter. The plane dips and pulls to the left.

"How are we doing up there, Syn?" I'm a little nervous.

"Sorry, sweetheart. It's going to be a bumpy ride." I hear in my ear. "Just so you know, that struck engine caught fire, but the pilot activated the motor's own fire-extinguishing gear. The fire's out, but the engine is toast."

"Do we have a landing approved?" I ask him, trying not to sound worried.

"We won't make it to our destination. We lost half our fuel in the fire. I'm hoping that we can clear some of the most mountainous tree-covered areas."

"I can't die before I've even had the chance to find him."

"We're not going to die today, Gray. Just hold on tight."

I open the sliding window so that I can see out. The sun is obscured by the storm clouds and the lightning is angry looking. I can barely make out the ground below. The airplane dips again and my stomach rolls.

"Syn, we are still moving too fast to land!"

"It's going to be a hard landing," he warns after a long moment.

I brace myself. All I can make out through the clouds is the tops of trees. I feel the landing gear finally swing down and the flail of the plane slings me forward against my seat belt.

Then everything happens as if in slow motion. Anything that's not tied down flies past me. My long hair is hanging in the air flowing by my face. Then a hard impact stops our movement.

For a split second, there is eerie silence, then I see water rushing by my window.

"Syn!" I yell. He doesn't answer. I quickly try to unbuckle, but it's jammed. Water is starting to enter the airplane. I stretch to open the overhead storage unit. After two attempts it pops open and I have to duck from the falling bags. I reach my knife and slice through the strap and stumble my way into the cockpit. Syn is slumped over in the co-pilot's chair and the pilot is unbuckling from his seat. I reach over and feel for a pulse. Thank God, he's alive.

"Are you okay?" I ask the pilot, Marc. Marc and I have been friends since we met in boot camp. He just got married and they are expecting their first child.

"I'm fine, just a little dazed. Let's get him out of here before this plane starts sinking further into the water. There is an emergency life raft in the closet in the back." He points in the direction.

It takes a few minutes to reach the closet because of the debris from the crash. I have to physically climb over metal carts that are overturned, as the water is getting deeper in the aisle. Inside the emergency closet, I find an inflatable life raft. Occupancy six. I'm familiar with how they work, so I don't waste time reading the instructions.

I grab my duffel bags with our weapons and I drag the bulky life raft to the emergency door. I unlatch it and water starts pouring inside. I tie the boat to a recessed cleat on the side of the plane and inflate it using the the battery powered attached motor. In moments, it's fully inflated.

I fight the waves of water rolling inside and Marc has Syn hoisted over his shoulder coming out of the cockpit. He has to hold onto the side of the plane with one hand to make his way to the exit.

Marc almost drops Syn as he lays him in the boat and instructs me to get in. I throw in the bags and carefully step into the boat beside Syn. He then joins us and unties the boat to drift away from the plane. As we float out, the wing of the plane is coming directly toward us.

"Get down," Marc yells. I duck just in time as it whips over us and starts to sink into the ocean.

The wind is strong and is pushing us hard. Rain is hammering down on us and the lightning is so close the thunder can be heard on top of the flash of light. I've been in many dangerous situations but never have I been so scared. The hair is standing up on my arms and the rain feels like bullets causing flesh wounds.

I can barely make out the shoreline. The waves are tossing us around and pushing us toward what looks like a jetty. If we hit them with the force of these waves, we will all be dead.

"I'm getting out to guide us," Marc yells, over the thunder. He jumps in and wraps a rope around his arm that is tied to the boat and starts swimming. We're taking on water and I'm splashing it out as fast I can. I have nothing to use to dump it out with. I jump out of the back of the boat and grab on so that I can kick and help us move faster. I finally feel the ground beneath me as a wave comes over me and knocks me down. Marc is already standing and pulling us. I get my bearings against the waves and push. We make it to the shore and I collapse into the sand, trying to catch my breath.

"We have to get out of the open!" I yell. I get to my feet and we drag the inflatable raft about two hundred yards into the trees. Syn is starting to stir. He has a gash on his forehead and blood combined with water is pouring down his face. He has to wipe it out of his eyes so that he can see.

"Where the hell are we?" Syn yells over the rain.

"We crash landed in the ocean, it was safer than trying to land in the jungles of China," Marc explains.

"Let me look at your head." I reach for Syn and he swats my hand away.

"I'm fine," he grumbles.

"Syn, just sit still and let me look, you were knocked out cold. You probably have a concussion." He lets me examine him this time. "You're going to need some stitches. I have a first aid kit in my duffel bag."

"Let's find some shelter first," Syn says, as he climbs out of the boat.

"The only shelter we're going to have until this storm lets up is this boat," Marc states as he lifts the heavy boat and pours the water out of it. We all sit-down under the boat that he is holding over us.

"We're sitting ducks under this damn bright yellow boat. We need to move as soon as the lightning slows," Syn states. The lightning pops overhead again as if to remind us.

23

About an hour later, Syn climbs to his feet. "I think it has slowed down enough for us to find somewhere safer," he suggests. Syn pulls his map out of his duffel bag. He lays it out on his lap. "This is where we were supposed to land." He points to a spot on the map. "This is where it appears we are now." He moves his finger to an area due east on the shoreline.

"By my calculations, we're twenty miles east of our entry point. We need to get over this mountain. It's a vertical climb. Once we get to the other side, the trees become dense. Both of these obstacles will slow us down, but once we make it to here," he points to a blue line on the map, "we can pick up speed following the river."

"Are you up to this, Syn?" I ask, pointing at his head.

"There isn't a choice. If we just sit here, then the Chinese will find us and they'll kill us. I'm sure by now they got word of a downed military plane. They may already be looking for us."

I pull out the first aid kit. "At least let me throw some stitches in your laceration, so the blood will quit running into your eyes." I take out lidocaine.

"We don't have time for that, just stitch it up," he growls.

Any other time I might enjoy causing him a little pain, but now is not one of them. "It will only take me two seconds."

Before he can even respond again, I have injected the area. Marc has threaded the surgical needle and hands it to me. Six stitches later, I have him closed up.

CHAPTER

Marc deflates the boat and hides it in some thick shrub. Syn grabs the duffel bag and points in the direction we need to go and takes the lead. It's steep and there's only a small area of trees that will hide us. The rest is rocky and barren.

We start walking toward our objective, once Marc catches up to us. Our march is brisk, but we're slowed by the increasing steepness. As we push toward the wooded part, it becomes more obvious that we're facing a mountain. We had a topographical map, that showed elevation, but we were now coming from a direction we hadn't prepared for.

"Syn, there's some rope in the bag. I think we're going to need it to anchor ourselves climbing this mountain," I tell him.

He stops and pulls the rope out and anchors it to himself, tied through his belt loops. He passes it to me next, and then I hand the end of the rope to Marc. With the three of us tied off securely together, we start our rough climb.

Syn is in the lead followed by me and then Marc. We take turns, alternating our climb in a pattern with two of us braced as the other climbs. I'm the lightest with two strong men on either end of my rope, so I have the best chance of finding solid holds to loop the rope to. Small rocks still break away with the weight of our climb. The rain clouds have all disappeared and the sun's blinding rays are shining directly in our eyes.

We've been climbing for over an hour now and the need for hydration increases with each step. "Syn, there is water in your bag," I tell him.

"Let's try and make it to those trees before we stop!" he yells down and points another two hundred yards in front of us.

I hear the backfire of a gun and then see a bullet ricocheted off a rock, narrowly missing me. We're caught completely out in the open. Syn starts climbing faster pulling on the rope, all but dragging me and Marc after him.

Marc missteps and pulls me with him. Bullets continue to ricochet around us. Syn is trying to pull us up the side of the mountain with the rope. Marc lets out a scream and I see his knee crumble and blood pooling on his pants. I grab the rope that anchors him to me and start pulling. Syn, in turn, is still pulling and dragging us up the rocky ledge.

I watch my cousin as he makes it into the trees and ties our rope off and pulls us even harder. I'm hanging on to my friend for dear life when I see him slump over with a direct hit to the chest. Syn tries to pull, but now he is pulling me and Marc's dead weight.

"Gray, you have to cut him off the line!" he yells.

"I can't. I can't leave him behind!" I cry out. Visions of his new bride flash before my eyes. Their wedding was only a few months ago. I attended with Steel and Ady. She was so excited to start her life with Marc and they were planning a big family. Then my mind suddenly flashes back to leaving soldiers behind in cages. I knew they were dead, but it was still a haunting scene. I'm frozen in place.

"Gray!"

I can't move.

"Gray, damn it! Look at me!" He is screaming, loudly.

I can't take my eyes off Marc.

"If you don't get your ass moving right now, we're all going to die on this mountain and Crew will never have a chance to be found. Now cut the damn line!"

My hands shake as I take the knife out of my boot. They're shaking so badly I almost drop the knife as I slice through the rope. "I'm so sorry," I cry as I watch Marc's lifeless body go crashing downward.

Syn yanks my body up the rocks scraping my elbows as he hauls me to safety. As soon as I'm up and hidden in the trees, he unzips the duffel bag and puts together my rifle.

"Get your shit together, right now. You're a better shot than me. I need you to pick off whoever is shooting at us." He hands my sniper rifle to me, the Accuracy International L11543 that I've had forever. I stare at it like it's a foreign object to me.

"Damn it, Gray! Now!" he yells.

Another bullet whizzes by me. I let my combat mode take over instead of the fear. I get low to the ground as he joins me with his rifle. Scanning the area with my scope, I catch a glimpse of a Chinese soldier peeking out from behind a tree. I pull the trigger and the soldier tumbles to the ground. Syn's rifle sounds and I see another soldier fall.

"Do you see anymore?" I whisper to him.

"No. But I'm betting that was their scouting team, and the rest of their pack is not too far behind them." He pulls me off the ground with him.

"We have to move up this mountain quickly!" He shoves our rifles back in the bag and ties the rope back around him. "I need you to stay focused and climb as quickly as you can," he commands.

Another thirty minutes and we finally make it to the top and sit behind a rock so that we are out of sight.

"I'm sorry, I froze back there. I just kept seeing the faces of the soldiers we left behind in those cages and Marc's wife." A tear rolls down my cheek and I brush it away.

27

"I'm sorry you had to cut him off. We'll send a team back for him," he says sadly. "He was a good guy."

"Steel." I try to sync with my cousin.

"You aren't going to be able to reach him out here." He touches my hand, "I promise we will return your friend home as soon as we can."

"Thanks."

"We have to get a move on it. The trees are thick and will provide us some protection." He pulls out a machete and takes the lead again, swinging hard on the vines.

"Watch out for poisonous snakes out here. The jungle is full of pit vipers, they're small, fast and highly aggressive. One bite and you'll die within thirty minutes. They have over three dozen kinds of poisonous snakes over here.

The Chinese soldiers would throw the pit vipers on us while we were sleeping. They would let us suffer in pure agony for fifteen minutes before they would administer the anti-venom. Their venom felt like lighter fluid going through your body."

He stops dead in his tracks and I run right into him. "Christ, Gray! Did they do that to you?" he looks angered.

I pull up my pant leg exposing my ankle and pull down my socks. There are two dark red puncture marks just above my ankle. The area around them is horribly scarred. I feel like explaining to him, "Pit viper venom is a haemotoxin and it affects the circulatory system, among other things. Their venom "digests" their prey from within, even before it is ingested; that's why viper bites leave behind nasty scars like these to those fortunate enough to survive. My leg still hurts every once in while..." I pull my sock back up and let my pant leg fall down again. "Just don't get bit," I suggest. "We don't have any anti-venom."

He lets out a growl and mumbles something about killing all those bastards but continues whacking at the branches to make a path for us. The brush and trees are so thick it takes us almost an hour to walk one mile.

"At this rate, we're not going to make it out of here before nightfall," I warn him, wiping the sweat out of my eyes.

"Let's make it as far as we can and we will set up camp."

"I'll take first watch. You haven't had any sleep, other than when you were knocked out cold."

"I won't argue with you on that, but we need to find food to keep our energy levels up."

The orange beams of the sun are setting behind the jungle. If I didn't hate this place so much, then I might think it was beautiful. "It will be dark soon."

"We can make camp here for the night. You gather some firewood and I'll go hunt something for us to eat. We'll want to keep the fire to a minimum, so don't start it until I come back."

I gather up a few large branches and twigs. I get sap from one of the trees to use as an ignitor. Syn makes it back to camp as the sun sets with a jungle rabbit in tow. I'm not surprised, China has a lot of rabbits, even in the jungle. Rabbits are hunted for their meat and fur. I've never batted an eye at killing an enemy, but I hate killing animals. He cleans it and cuts it up, while I start the fire.

As soon as we are done eating, I stomp at the embers left from the fire. "Go to sleep, Syn. I'll wake you in six hours." I have my rifle tucked at my side as he curls up to keep warm.

The stillness of the night makes my mind run back to the night before our team was captured.

Crew had received word that there were two downed pilots that were captured and being held in a small village. Crew assigned eight of our soldiers for the rescue mission. I was not included, but I was determined to go with him.

"I want to go with you," I protested as I snuggled into his bare chest.

"Not this time. I have a bad feeling about this mission." He rubbed my back and reached for his pocket watch that was sitting on a makeshift nightstand. He took it between his fingers and rubbed the outside of it. I'd seen him do that many times before and he always placed it in his pocket, but that time, he handed it to me.

"My father carried this with him until the day he died. He left it to me in his Will, along with a note explaining its importance."

I sat up to examine it closer. It was silver and gold and you could see the worn metal where fingers prints had rubbed off some of the grooves in it. I opened the metal locket that held it together. The hands didn't move. "It doesn't work?"

"The note my father wrote me said that it was my great-great grandfathers. His wife had given it to him on their wedding day. Their initials use to be on the inside." He pointed to where you can see what looked like it used to be the curl of a C. "They have worn off over the years," he explained.

"When he died his son made the time stop in honor of his father. He said that he was one of the greatest men he had ever known and that time stood still for him that day. He's handed it down along with his story for generations," he sat up to face me, "I want you to keep it for me."

"What? No!" I was freaking out about the mission. He knew something about it that he wasn't telling me.

"Please, don't fight me on this. You can give it back to me when we're in the states." He squeezed my hand around it and laid back down. "There is one other thing I need from you."

"What is it?" I rubbed his bare chest.

He got out of bed and walked over to his desk and pulled out a file and returned to sit on the bed. "I don't have any family. My adoptive parents were already up in age when they brought me home. They've been gone for many years now and I have no siblings. If something were to happen to me, I have no one to speak for me. I want you to be my Power of Attorney and my Medical Surrogate." He handed me the papers from the file with a pen.

"You are scaring the shit of me. Why now?"

"I haven't had anyone for a very long time. Now, I have you. You know it's something we all have signed when we joined the military. I've left mine blank all these years."

I knew he was right, Syn was listed on my form. I didn't want my parents to have to make hard decisions for me. I tapped the pen on the paper a few times and then I signed it. He took it and placed it on the nightstand and laid back down, taking me with him. "Thank you," he said, but there was still stress in his smile, which made me uneasy.

"Now that you've thoroughly made me nervous about this mission, I definitely want to go on it with you. I can scout ahead." I propped myself up on my elbows to look at him.

"I'd rather you wouldn't, in fact, I'd feel better if you got out of the Army altogether." He scowled at me and sat up.

"Wait! What? You've never mentioned this before. Besides, I like my job and I'm pretty damn good at it." I sat up next to him and kissed his shoulder.

"You're damn good at your job, we both know that—but I can't stand seeing you put yourself in danger, over and over. I don't know what I'd do if I lost you." He turned and kissed me softly. "I love you and the stronger our bond becomes, the less I want you doing this."

"What about you? I don't like you putting yourself in danger either."

"I've been thinking about that too. I'll make this my last mission. Let's go back to the states, get married and start a family."

I was totally floored by his words. We'd never discussed any life beyond the military. "Is that really what you want?" My eyes were locked on his.

"Yes, more than anything. I want to spend the rest of my days making love to you and raising our rug rats." He kissed me again and pushed me back on the bed as he straddled over me. His hands roamed my body.

"What is it that you want, baby?"

"What if I want your fingers to continue what they're doing?"

He laughed. "Will you marry me?"

"On one condition," I said, as I moaned in pleasure.

He bit my lip. "What might that be?"

"If you let me go on this one last mission with you, then I'll hang up my rifle. I'll let you put a ring on my finger," I moaned again.

"As long as we can start making those babies right now," he added.

I hear a noise a few feet out. I stand up and put my night goggles on. I look in the direction of where I heard the noise. A monkey is climbing a tree, nothing else. I settle back down against the tree to keep watch.

Crew never knew we made a baby that night. I didn't find out until after I had been beaten.

I'd lost track of time being held in those cages. Almost three months after our capture, I was being tortured for information and when I didn't give them an answer, one of my torturers repeatedly kicked me in the stomach. When he threw me back in the cage that night I started hemorrhaging.

Crew screamed for help until they finally sent someone in to look at me. They drug me by the hair into this cold room and laid me on a table. They sent in a butcher to look at me. I could only make out a few words, but baby, that I understood clearly.

I almost died from what that monster did to me. I didn't find out until after I was rescued, that I would never be able to have children again. The butcher had ripped everything out of me. I don't know why he didn't just let me die. He doctored me back up and threw me back in the cage three days later.

I was so numb on the inside, I couldn't tell Crew what happened. I was afraid he would go berserk and they'd kill him.

Looking back, that might've been better than the torture he received. I held out hope of a rescue, that came a little too late.

Sometimes I would lie in that cage and dream about the baby that we lost. Crew would've been a wonderful father. He told me he wanted a daughter that looked just like me. I would've given him anything he wanted.

He was a tough leader, but his love for me was so tender and intimate. I loved both sides of him. His men respected him, myself included, but I had a part of him that he shared with no other person. I owned him as much as he owned me.

We were lying next to each other in our cages late one night—grateful to be able to just touch each other. We said our made up wedding vows to one another. His words were so real to me, I fell in love with him all over again. This was my most cherished moment with him. It was unequaled in emotion to anything I had ever experienced with him before. In my heart, we were husband and wife.

"Wake up, Syn." I gently shake him.

He slowly rolls over and stretches. "Is it time already?"

"Yeah, I need some sleep." I curl into a ball for warmth.

"Get some rest, I'll wake you at sunrise and we'll get a move on it," he says.

I'm so exhausted that I fall right to sleep and don't even dream—which I'm thankful for because I'm not sure how I would deal with seeing Crew in my dreams again. Especially, if they were dreams of his torment like they used to be when I first got back. My dreams were always haunted. All I wanted to dream about now were the good times I had with him.

"Hey, sweetheart. Wake up, we need to get moving," Syn says, as he shakes me lightly.

"I'm up…I'm up," I say, as I'm trying to shake off sleep. I get up and rub the leaves off of my fatigues.

He hands me some water. "It's going to take us another couple of hours to make it to the river. Then we should be able to move pretty quickly. I just hope our team hasn't left without us," he adds.

We're already hours late. Our team could have left without us. I wouldn't blame them. This mission is on a timetable, after all. If they had been monitoring Chinese broadcasts, they may even heard about our crashed plane. I can't tell any of this to Syn, I don't want to discourage him. He's as driven as I am, but I'm exhausted. I need his strength. Maybe he knows it too but doesn't want to mention it either.

"Let's get started then. At least we seemed to have lost the Chinese soldiers that were chasing us."

"I hope you're right," he hikes a duffel bag on his shoulder and hands me the other one.

Several grueling hours later, we finally make it to a clearing and can see the river. "I'm going to go ahead and scope out the area and make sure there are no unfriendlies waiting for us." He puts down his bag.

I put mine down, too. I pull my rifle out just in case he runs into any trouble. I watch and scan the area as he moves toward the water. I don't see any movement other than the wind blowing in the trees. He makes it to the water and waves for me to join him. I put my rifle back in the bag, grab our things, and move toward him.

When I reach him, he takes one of the bags and pulls out the map. "We need to head down the river until we come to this point." He has his finger on the spot on the map. "Once we get there, we'll need to head due west. A team of soldiers should be waiting for us. The river has some rough white water areas that we're going to have to maneuver around."

Both of us turn as we hear gunfire in the distance. "Run!" he yells.

We both take off running, trying to avoid the rocks. I look behind us and see several Chinese soldiers heading for the river, pointing at us. I can hear the white waters in front of us.

"Syn, we need to get in the water up ahead or they are going to kill us!" I yell at him. He shifts his direction straight to the rapids and I'm right on his heels. We stop momentarily to secure our bags and hear gunfire again. The water ahead is really rough, but it is our only option.

"Keep your feet up, don't let them drag and get caught on the rocks," he instructs.

"I'll see you down the river," I say and we both jump as a closer round of gunfire is heard.

I come up gasping for air as the heavy bags try to pull me under. Then I'm caught in the current that is brutally pushing me forward. I bounce off a few rocks. I can see Syn in front of me battling the rapids. I hit a deep area and it sucks me under. I have no choice but to remove my bag before it drowns me. I sputter once I reach the surface and I hear Syn calling my name. I swim to reach him and he grabs me by the shoulder pulling me out. He sees my bag under the water and he jumps in after it as I lay in the grass trying to catch my breath.

"No time for that, sweetheart. Get your ass up and move!" He points down the river again.

We run for a couple miles before we come to our outlet. We don't break pace as we turn into the jungle. I hear Syn trying to link with the soldiers. Two men come out from behind the trees in the distance with their guns out and ready.

We both stop dead in our tracks, and Syn starts rattling off orders for them to stand down. We reach them and he directs them to watch for the Chinese behind us. They link in for back up and point us in the direction of the camp.

We make it into the captain's tent before either one of us stops to take a breather. The CO's name is Captain Dodge.

"Let me do the talking," he says in my ear.

I listen as Captain Dodge updates Syn on the soldiers that were found. Since we were delayed, they went in without us to rescue them. He tells him that they were near death, but have since been shipped to a military base. They would have a long recovery, but physically they should be fine. Mentally is another story.

Syn pulls the map out of his bag and shows him the area the other soldiers are more than likely being held, because of the terrain. It's about an hour hike on foot and the area is heavily booby trapped. There are a few Chinese left in a hut, guarding the area.

He tells Syn that he has a team of six soldiers to send with us, one is a medic. Another transport team will meet us at the extraction location, but they're not scheduled to make it there until tomorrow.

"Syn—" I start to tell him that I don't want to wait another day, but he cuts me off.

"We'll get some food and water and head out tonight. I want the advantage of darkness in our favor. They won't expect anyone to attack them at night."

I sigh. There is no point in arguing. He's right, of course.

"I don't miss the military food," I say as I pick at my food.

"Eat it anyway," Syn says as he devours his food.

"Do you really think we'll find him?" I whisper.

"If he's out there, then we'll find him." He gives me a soft look.

"Do you think we'll get to him tonight?"

"Our goal tonight is to secure the area. In the morning, we'll be able to search the area for any underground caverns."

"I hate the thought of him or any other soldier being in there even one more night," I admit sadly.

He puts his hand on my shoulder. "I promise we will get to them as soon as humanly possible."

"Thanks." I smile weakly at him.

"When we're done here, why don't you try to get a little rest?" He returns to eating.

I eat what I can, then head out to find a place to lay down. One of the soldiers lets me borrow his tent and his makeshift shower. I wash quickly in the cold water and curl up on the cot.

I drift off and I see Crew's face.

It was the night our team was captured. We'd rushed into the village to save the two captured pilots. I had climbed on the roof of one of the buildings across from where they were being held.

The team made it in safely, but before they could come back out, the building was surrounded by enemy soldiers. I started picking them off one by one, but there were too many of them. I took out eight of them, but another eight remained.

I linked with Crew to let him know that they'd entered the building and I was headed down. He barked a harsh "No!" and ordered me to stay put and to stay out of sight.

A few minutes later our team emerged from the building with the Chinese soldiers aiming guns at their heads. Their leader started yelling for me to come out or he would start killing them one by one.

"Don't move," Crew gritted out.

"Crew, I—"

"You have your orders."

Before I could respond, I heard the shot. Their leader killed one of the pilots they'd been holding captive.

He yelled out again and grabbed Crew. He had him kneel on the ground, as he squatted for cover behind him.

"I'll put a bullet through his head on the count of ten."

He was well hidden behind Crew. I couldn't get a clear shot of him without risking killing Crew, too.

He started his count.

"One!"

"Don't do it, Gray," Crew whispered.

"Two!"

"I can't just let him kill you." Tears clouded my eyes.

"Three!"

"When he shoots me and I fall forward, take him out," he said quietly.

"Four!"

"Crew—" I choked out his name.

"Five!"

"I love you, baby," he whispered.

"Six!"

"I love you, too," I sobbed again.

"Seven!"

"Hold strong, Sniper." He breathed in deep.

"Eight!"

Tears flooded my vision.

"Nine!"

"I'm sorry, Crew," I choked one last time.

I stood up and threw my rifle over the rooftop, to the ground. I could see the anger on Crew's face. "I'm sorry, I couldn't let you die," I whispered again.

I saw him close his eyes tight. "You have no idea what they will do to a woman." I heard the anguish in his voice. He was willing to die for me, but I couldn't let him. I was willing to risk whatever they had planned to save the man I loved. Little did I know that what they'd planned for all of us was worse than death. Before I let them take me, I stashed the pocket watch Crew had given me to hold. I knew they would take everything from me. I planned to come back for it when I escaped.

Pieces of Gray

The Chinese soldiers chained us all up together and lead us deep into the jungle. Crew was chained to the front and I was at the end.

He kept trying to talk to me through his link but one of the soldiers hit him on the side of the head with his rifle and the link disconnected. I could see blood running down his neck and he moved a little slower. I tried to move faster and pass the other soldiers to get to him, but one of the captors pointed a gun to my head and motioned for me to get back in line.

When we finally reached our destination in the middle of the jungle they threw us in cages. I felt lucky that my cage was butted up next to Crew's. I wanted to touch him, but I stayed huddled in my corner until there were no guards hovering over us. I didn't want them to see that I was attached to one of them. I thought it might save Crew from further harm. At night when the guards fell asleep, we would both cling to each other through our cages. It made me feel safe in a dangerous place.

I bolt up out of sleep, soaked in sweat. I'm so glad I woke up before I had to relive our torture.

Watching the powerful man that I loved be beat, isn't something I want to ever relive again. It took months and lots of therapy before I could sleep without nightmares.

I shower again, change clothes, and set out to find Syn. He's asleep in the captain's quarters. I sit on the ground next to him and watch him. I don't want to be alone right now, and he has always been a comfort to me. He can be a royal pain in the ass, but he was my rock when I came back home. He made me feel safe again. He never forced me to talk about what happened to me. He waited patiently and he was there when I finally broke down.He's my cousin, but I consider him my best friend.

CHAPTER

4

"Hey," Syn says to wake me.

"I must've drifted off."

"You okay?" he looks concerned.

"Yeah, I'm fine, I just didn't want to be alone," I say quietly and climb off the floor running my hands down my pants.

"Are you sure you want to do this? There's no telling what kind of conditions we're going to find in those caves."

"There's no way in hell I'm staying behind." I grab my gear off the ground.

"I wish you would reconsider and let my team handle it," he huffs out.

I step up close to him. "I don't care what we find, but I need to be there if Crew is alive. I am part of your team."

"Okay," he concedes holding his hands in the air. "Let's go then."

By the time we arrive, the captain has already gathered the soldiers that are going with us in a huddle in the middle of the camp. Syn takes over and reviews the plan with each of them.

"Good luck," Captain Dodge tells us as we leave.

I scout ahead with one other soldier, while two hang behind with my cousin. The rest of the soldiers stay within steps of one another. Each one of us is on alert and armed. The sun makes its final descent and we all put our night goggles on.

I make it to just outside the hut before anyone else. I see a Chinese soldier on the porch asleep in a chair. It's dark inside the hut.

"Syn, there is a soldier asleep on the porch," I whisper into my link.

"Take him out before we get there," he orders.

I place the silencer on my rifle and take aim. He slumps over in the chair and no one is the wiser. "Target taken care of," I inform Syn.

"Don't get any closer until we get there."

"Roger that," I respond and hold my ground.

A few minutes later, Syn and his team join me. "You two stay out here," he commands. "The rest of you I want to surround that hut. I want every Chinese soldier inside dead except for one. We need to interrogate one of them to confirm our suspicions. Gray, you stick next to me," he orders.

He holds my arm until all the men are in place. "Let them take care of this part."

I nod my head and move to the hut. He motions for his men to enter. Four enemies are inside and startle awake when we move inside. Three of them are killed immediately before they can react. The fourth one still alive is backed into a corner with his hands in the air.

"Tie him up," Syn commands.

Two of the team members grab him and place him in a chair in the middle of the room. We remove our goggles and turn on the light. Syn starts questioning him as I move around the room. There are books and playing cards on an old worn out desk. There's a pile of porn magazines on the corner. I open the single desk drawer and rummage through it.

In the very back of the drawer, I find some photos. I take them out and flip through each one of them. They're pictures of soldiers being tortured. Their heads are covered with black hoods. Every one of the men is naked and thin.

Crew has a tattoo of the Roman numeral three with 13 stars in a circle around it on his right upper arm. I remember him telling me about it.

The stars represent the thirteen original colonies and the Roman numeral represents that the king's army was defeated by a resistance that never amounted to more than three percent of the colonial population. It was called the three percenters.

I can see a shadow of a tattoo on one of the men, but I can't make it out. A lot of soldiers have arm tattoos. His body is so thin, I wouldn't recognize it. It could be him, though. My heart nearly stops with the possibility.

I'm taken over by a surge of anger. I draw my pistol from my hip holster and rush over to the Chinese soldier and point it at his head.

"What are you doing, Gray?" Syn snaps.

"Look at these pictures!" I yell as I shove them in front of our prisoner's face.

He starts speaking in Chinese, but I don't understand a word he is saying.

"English, damn it! I know you know the language!" I'm in a rage.

"Calm down, Gray. Let me see the pictures." Syn is trying to bring me down before I put a bullet in our captive's head. He slowly takes them from me, but I don't lower my weapon.

He squints at the pictures. "Do you think one of these could be him?"

I point to the one with the tattoo on his shoulder. "This might be him."

He hands it to the Chinese soldier. "Is this man still alive?" he asks, but the soldier says nothing. Syn pulls his arm back and hits him in the face. Blood is pooling at the corner of his mouth.

"If you don't answer me, then I'm going to let her question you. I'm sure she learned some skills from being tortured by you and your men."

He glances at the picture and shakes his head yes.

I launch myself at him, but Syn catches me right before I can get my hands on him.

"That's not how this is going to go down, Gray. We still need him alive to show us the exact location of the underground cages. I can only guess, but he can take us right to them," he says calmly. "Now, stand down" he warns me.

I know he's right, I have to keep my cool. I holster my gun and walk back over to the desk.

Syn gets down in his face. "Come daylight, you're going to take me to him. Do you understand me?" He responds with a nod.

I stop halfway to the desk and wheel back around. "Why aren't we going now?" I demand.

"You know as well as I do that there could be more of them in the jungle and the underground cages are going to be pitch black. We have to go in the morning, so we don't risk any of our men." He walks over to me. "You have to trust me," he whispers. I nod and he turns toward his men. "I want four on the perimeter, and you on the porch," he points to each of them.

"Where do you want me?" I ask him.

"You're not to leave my sight," he orders.

I think he knows that I would take off and start searching on my own—if given the chance. I want to be angry with him, but he's right. I don't want to risk any of these soldier's lives unnecessarily.

He walks up and stares into my eyes. "Did I make myself clear?"

I nod my head. He takes my chin and holds it up. "If he is out there, then we'll find him and bring him home." He hands back the picture I'd found. I clutch it desperately.

A single tear rolls down my face. "This could really be him..." My voice breaks off as I stare at the picture. Is it wishful thinking that the more I stare at it, the more certain I become?

"I believe you. But I need you to rest so that you're ready first thing in the morning."

I lay down on a cot in the corner of the room, but rest doesn't come. I have let my thoughts and fears run rampant. What if Crew hates me for leaving him behind? I thought he was dead, but did he know that? I have no idea what those bastards told him. How can he possibly be the same man after all these years?

It took me months for my mind to return to normal, but my heart never did. I still ache for him. I loved everything about him. He was strong, yet soft and sweet. His mind was brilliant. The sex was mind-blowing—but even if you took that away—I would've loved him anyway.

He made me feel cherished in every possible way. I would give anything to have him back and I'll love him regardless of who he is now. I know he would do the same for me. A small part of me prays that it isn't him in the picture. That man's life has had to be hell. I know all too well that there are things that are worse than death.

Dawn comes early. Syn makes sure all his men have eaten and drank plenty of water. He even feeds the prisoner.

It infuriates me when I think about how little they fed us. Twice a week they would throw raw fish in our cages and sometimes stale bread. Sometimes we threw those scraps back up or got sick from them. They would always provide us plenty of water because God forbid we died from thirst. They seemed to know exactly how little food we could survive off of and how long in between days we could go without food. It makes me so angry that I walk over and yank the water bottle out of his mouth.

"Gray, what the hell are you doing?" Syn snaps. "That's not how we treat prisoners."

"Do you think he gave a shit whether or not our soldiers were thirsty or hungry?" I snap back.

"I —" he starts to say.

"Don't!" I yell. "You have no idea what they did to us or what they are still doing to our POW's."

He opens his mouth to say something but thinks better of it.

He turns from me without a word. He unties the prisoner from the chair and hauls him up to stand. Syn carefully checks the prisoner's wrist bindings, before he warns him, "let's go before I change my mind and let her kill your sorry ass."

I grab my duffel bag and follow Syn and the prisoner out to the porch. Syn gives some quick orders and the soldiers disperse. He shoves the prisoner down the steps and orders him to lead the way. I see our men spread out into the jungle.

About a half-mile in, we hear gunfire and take cover behind trees. I pull out my sniper rifle and start searching, in a defensive crouch.

I link up with the soldiers in our unit and warn them where I've spotted the Chinese soldiers hiding. They are able to sneak up behind them and take them out.

Just to be sure, I start looking around with my rifle scope. I spot another Chinese soldier taking aim at one of our soldiers through his own sniper rifle. I squeeze the trigger of my gun and watch him fall. Someday, I know that same fate could happen to me, but I always push that thought aside.

I hear a tree whip behind me and watch as one of our soldier's steps into a trap. He lets out a startled yelp as his feet are yanked out from under him. In another moment, he's hanging upside down and swinging by feet. At least he didn't scream and give away our position. I hear something else, a whirring sound.

I quickly jump up and run straight at him, swinging his body out of the way of an arrow. It just barely misses him. I pull him down, putting all my weight into it. Once he's down, I cut the ropes around his feet that kept him hanging upside down. I ask in a whisper if he can walk. He nods and gets to his feet, but gives me a nod of thanks.

Syn gives the all clear for us to continue. We slowly make it to where the Chinese soldiers have fallen. Syn shoves our prisoner forward. "What is it they were protecting? Show me now!" He pulls out his gun and presses it to the back of the man's head. The prisoner points to an area covered in brush. I walk over and pull it down. There is a cave opening. I point a light into it and it leads downward. It looks deep.

I don't want to yell and possibly be heard by any enemy soldiers that could be hiding down there. I hurry back and report to Syn, "This has to be it."

"I want the two of you out here securing the entrance," Syn gives hasty orders and pointing to a pair of our team. "And I want you two to take the lead, and one of you to keep your eyes on this asshole," he orders pointing at the other three in turn.

Syn pushes the captive toward the soldier who'll guard him. "If this asshole even flinches, or does anything suspicious, kill him," he says flatly. The soldier nods back at Syn and grabs ahold of the prisoner, keeping his weapon on him with the other hand.

CHAPTER

T he rest of us, including the medic, slowly enter the cave with our flashlights outstretched. The stench is horrific. It smells of dead fish and feces. It brings back flashes of my prison.

Now more than ever, I am certain this is the right place.

The smell makes one of the soldiers vomit. He does so quietly, muffling his spewing mouth with a hand. The rest of us wait for him to get himself together. There's no shame in it, we've all had moments our stomachs reacted to some sight or smell. As soon as he's done, he stands and gives a nod. We press on as if nothing had happened.

The cold rock walls are covered in a wet, mossy plant and dangerously slippery to the touch. The man-made steps leading downward into darkness are narrow and winding. We all remain very quiet as we move, it's a remote possibility there are other Chinese soldiers down there guarding the prisoners. Some people really CAN get used to the smell of anything.

The potent stench only becomes stronger as we make it to the bottom of the stairs.

Syn shines his light down a long, dark corridor. I can make out six cells. We press forward. Syn shines his light in the first cell and it's completely empty.

There are scratches in the far wall like counting marks. I stop a few moments and mentally tally them up. There are eight hundred and twenty-five marks. That means there was someone in this hell hole for two years and two months. That's almost the exact amount of time I have been free from my prison.

The second cell has a bare cot in the corner, but no sign of life. The third one has dried fish bones piled in a corner and a single chair that sits in the middle of the cell. The fourth one turns my stomach. There is a skeleton laying in the middle with binds still on the wrists and ankles. The fifth one has a soldier laying on his cot.

His eyes are fixed to the ceiling. Syn yells out to him, but there is no response. I hear a noise coming from the sixth cell at the sound of Syn's voice. I pass Syn and shine my light into the cell and there is a man curled up in the corner. He is naked and his hair hangs long down over his body. I see him lift his head upward off of his knees.

"Syn, this one is alive!" I yell and frantically feel the walls around me for a key.

"There," the medic says as he shines the light two feet above my head.

I jump up to grab the ring from its nail. Shakily, I put the key in the hole. "It's okay, you're safe now. We're going to get you out of here." As I open the door, Syn steps in front of me.

"Let me." His eyes are pleading. I nod and let him pass. I hand the keys to another soldier to check on the other prisoner in the cell next to him.

Cautiously, Syn broaches the man sitting in the corner. He squats in front of him. "My name is Captain Jaxsyn Nolan with the United States Army. We've come to get you out of here."

The man doesn't say anything, he lays his head back down on his knees. I hear the medic say that the soldier in the fifth cell is barely alive as he enters the sixth cell.

"Soldier, can I have our medic check you out?" Syn asks quietly.

His voice is soft and raspy. "Just let me die."

"We didn't come all this way to let you die. Please, let us help you," Syn pleads.

The soldier lays flat on the floor and the medic gets his bag out and starts assessing him.

"Get some clothes for this soldier out of my bag," Syn barks at me.

The soldier looks tall and emaciated, Syn is much shorter but I'm sure his clothes are going to drown him. I pull a pair of army pants and a t-shirt out of his bag. I hear the medic ask him his name, but he doesn't answer.

"We're going to need to build a make-shift gurney to get him out of here, Sir. He is too weak to walk." He leans into Syn's ear and I hear him whisper about the first man we found, "Another day and he would have been dead."

Syn links with the soldiers outside and instructs them to work on building two gurneys and tells them we will be leaving within the hour.

I grab some water and a protein bar out of my bag and hand the clothes to Syn. The medic helps the soldier sit back up. His hair is obscuring his face. I sit down on the cold damp floor next to him.

"Here's some water and food," I say softly, trying not to frighten him.

He grabs both of them from me and rips into the bar. He coughs and downs the water. I watch as it drips into his beard. As he lifts his head, I see the pain on his face. His beard is almost as long as his hair and it's difficult to see what he looks like.

"I have some clothes for you. Can I help you get dressed?"

His gravelly voice sounds a little louder this time. "I haven't had clothes on in years."

Syn and the medic help him off the ground and hold him up as his knees try to collapse. I gather up each pant leg and slip them over his feet and pull them up to his waist. They hang on him. My eyes start to tear at the thought of how much this man has suffered. I get behind him and gather his matted hair in my hands. Syn maneuvers his head into the shirt. I let his hair fall and walk to place his arm in the sleeve and as I lift his arm I see his tattoo. Crew's tattoo. I gasp and fall backward. The movement startles him and he breaks free of Syn and the medic, and curls into a ball on the floor.

"What is it?" Syn asks me.

"It's...it's him." My voice cracks. How the hell could I have not recognized him? Even face to face?

"Are you sure?" Syn isn't convinced.

I point to his tattoo and tears are streaming down my face.

Syn gets down on the floor with him. "Are you Captain Kell Crew?"

He sits up and faces Syn. "I haven't heard my name in so long, I had almost forgotten it," he grates out almost in pain.

I crawl on the floor to sit in front of him."It's me, Gray."

He looks up and his eyes search mine. I tentatively place my hand on his.

"Gray?" he rasps and his eyes squint. "I thought you were dead?"

"No, I was rescued. I...I thought you were dead," I sob.

"You left me here?" He removes his hand from mine.

"They told me you had died. I searched for you when they found us." I reach for his face but hear gunfire.

Syn starts talking on his link, giving orders to get the makeshift gurneys down here now and to take out whoever is shooting at them. A few minutes later, several soldiers enter the cave with the gurneys. The medic and I help Crew get onto it and then the other soldier onto the other one.

Pieces of Gray

"Sir, we took out two more Chinese soldiers. I'm sure they have backup on the way. We need to get the hell out of here," he tells Syn.

"Get them out of here now. Gray, grab your rifle and scout out ahead of us," he orders.

"But —"

"Do as you're told!" He points to my bags.

I wipe the tears from my face and go into sniper mode. I grab my bags and my rifle and head up the narrow stairs into daylight. Two of our soldiers go out with me and one stays behind with our prisoner. The sight of him sends me into a rage.

"Keep that bastard away from me or I will kill him," I snap at the soldier. I head to the hilly area so that I can secure the perimeter. I look around through my scope but I don't see anything other than our other soldiers setting up.

I point my scope to the cave as I see Syn emerging with our soldiers carrying the gurney with Crew on it. He shields his eyes from the sun as if he hasn't seen it in years.

Syn and the men stop to talk to the soldier who is holding our prisoner. Then in slow motion, I watch as Crew steals Syn's sidearm pistol from his hip holster. No one else but me sees him aim it at the Chinese soldier and pull the trigger.

Our captive falls lifeless to the ground. The medic scrambles to get to him, but I hear Syn order him to stop. Syn turns back to Crew, palm out. Crew gives his weapon back without further incident.

"Syn!" I bark in my link.

"Keep your ground, don't move and don't hesitate," he calmly says back to me.

My heart breaks for Crew. Part of me is happy that he got to kill one of his captors, the other part of me is sad that he will have so much pain to work through.

My attention is grabbed when I spot movement about two hundred feet out. I take aim and start shooting. I take out three before they even know what hit them. They dive for cover and two more are taken out by our other soldiers.

"Syn, it's clear to the west. Get them out of here! I'll take care of the rest of the hostiles and meet you at the extraction point."

"Do you remember how to get there?"

"You put a map in my bag. I'll find it. Now, get them out of here!"

"One hour, Gray. That's all the time we have. I've already linked up with the helicopter pilot. Get there and don't be late!"

He orders one of the other soldiers to stay behind with me, another sniper named Sam. We met at sniper school. Syn and the other men take off with Crew and the other soldiers.

I lay out a line of gunfire to cover them. I don't stop until they're out of plain sight.

My link goes off with Sam's voice in my ear. "There's at least six more holed up on the east side of the cave."

"Keep them in your scope. I'm going to climb down and circle around behind them."

"Roger that."

I crawl down the backside of the hill and make my way through the dense trees to the east. I hear a single shot.

"One down," I hear in my ear.

Gunfire returns and I take off running. I see an enemy soldier hiding behind a tree. I take him out, but not before I hear Sam cry out in pain in my ear. "I've been hit in the leg!"

"I'm coming, hold your ground."

I take out three more. I know there is at least one more here. I get down on the ground and start my sniper crawl. I make it in only a few feet before I hear a noise above me. I turn over as he jumps out of a tree and lands on top of me.

My rifle goes flying. He has his knife aimed at my throat. Both of my hands are on his wrists trying to hold him off. His sweat drips into my eyes and he's yelling something in Chinese.

His knife is within an inch of my throat when he suddenly slumps on top of me. I manage to catch the knife but not before it slices across my shoulder with the weight of his body falling on me. Sam is pulling him off of me.

When I get up off the ground, I can see that the sniper stabbed him in the back of the neck.

"Is that all six of them?" He asks as blood is soaking through his pant leg.

"Yes, I answer as I pull the belt off the Chinese soldier. I place it around Sam's leg making a tourniquet to stop the bleeding. Then I rub my hand across my shoulder and decide that mine is only a flesh wound.

"We need to get the hell out of here, now!" I gather my rifle and bag, throw it over my shoulder. I grab Sam under his shoulder to help support him. "Thanks for saving my ass by the way."

"You're saving my ass now, so we're even," he said as he smiles at me.

"There is something I still need to do before we leave this place." I dig through my duffel bag and find a spektum. It's an explosive device the size of a large marble. It's a micro-grenade, but the damage it causes is enormous. "I have to destroy that cave. They're never going to use it again. Cover me in case we didn't get them all." I lean him against a tree, then run as fast as I can to the cave entrance. I throw the spektum down the stairs and run back to the other sniper.

I support his weight again and we take off. He hops on one leg to try to help pick up our speed. I hear his pain every time he hits the ground, but he doesn't complain. We stop at the water line to rest. I help him to sit down on a large rock. I take out the remote and detonate the spektum. The explosion is immediate. We duck from flying debris. That will be a good distraction, to draw enemy attention away from Syn and Crew, and also from me and Sam. Like Crew, I also needed this small measure of revenge.

We watch for a moment and tears fill my eyes. I quickly wipe them away, because I know all of China probably heard the explosion.The rumbling is still going, the explosion was much louder than I'd expected. "We really have to get out of here."

"How much further?"

I dig the map out of my bag. "We need to head east down the river, another ten minutes or so. Then, we should meet up with them. I look around and find him a large enough stick that he can lean on as he walks. He takes it and gets up right away and starts down the river.

Five minutes into our hike, I hear the roar of the helicopter blades. "Hurry up, soldier or they are going to leave us behind." He abandons the stick and I help him again. We move almost at a run. We make the clearing, and I see Syn with all his tactical gear on standing in front of the opening to the helicopter. I link up with him hoping he can hear me over the roaring blades. "Sam's hurt."

He looks in our direction and then instructs another soldier to come help us. He helps me get the injured soldier into the chopper and I barely make it in before it takes off.

"You okay?" Syn yells and points to the blood on my shoulder.

"Just a scratch. How is Crew?" I look over and the medic is now working on Sam's injured leg.

"Miraculously, the medic was able to start an IV on him. The fluids will do him some good. He is extremely weak and his vitals are unstable. As soon as we land, we're going to have him put on a military medical plane to take him to the nearest base, which is Portland. Unfortunately, the other soldier died as we made it to the plane. We attempted CPR, but he was too far gone. I guess the strain of moving him..." His voice trails off and ends in a scowl.

I touch Syn's hand. "I'm so sorry we didn't get to him in time. I want to go with Crew."

"You know that's not allowed. We have to go through debriefing. We'll meet up with him as soon as we can. I synched with General Maynard, he is flying both of our parents to Portland. They'll get there long before us."

"But he doesn't know any of them."

"They're going for you. Mom will be able to get details on his condition for us." He squeezes my hand.

"I just wish I could be there."

"I know. We'll get there soon enough. We're going to meet all of them at Steel's place since it's empty right now."

I get out of my seat and go lay beside Crew who is sleeping. I'm sure the medic gave him enough drugs to keep him comfortable for the flight home. I fall asleep almost immediately.

This time the nightmares don't come.

CHAPTER

O ur debriefing lasted almost a week. During that time we were able to attend the military funeral of the other soldier we brought back. His name was Private Daniel Davis. He was only twenty-eight years old. His only living relative is his twin brother, Douglas. Syn and I both had a chance to speak with him privately. Douglas glared at Syn and me during the entire funeral. I feel bad for his loss, it could so easily have been Crew we were burying.

I'm dying to go see Crew. Our first stop is Steel's fortress. He and Ady won't be home from their honeymoon for another week. We pull into the long drive to see my dad and Uncle Kyren working in the garden. Acheron and Styxx, Steel's lovable Pit Bulls are the first to greet us. As soon as my dad sees me, he puts down the hoe and runs over to me, engulfing me in a huge hug.

"I'm so glad you're both back."

"Me too, Dad."

As soon as he lets go of me, Uncle Kyren sneaks in for a hug. "Your Aunt Brogan and your mom are waiting inside to update you on Crew," he says softly.

"What about me? I'm chopped liver in comparison to her, I suppose," Syn says laughing, as he hugs both of them.

We get inside and I smell my favorite peanut butter cookies baking. "Looks like the two of you have been up to no good," I say as I see Aunt Brogan and my mom in aprons and flour on their faces.

"You're back. Oh thank God," my mom says as she rounds the counter and hugs me.

"You've made my favorite cookies!" A tear rolls down my cheek. Aunt Brogan joins our hug.

"These are the best thing I've eaten in weeks," Syn says with a mouthful of cookies. We all laugh at him.

"Aunt Brogan, I know I just walked in the door, but what can you tell me about Crew?"

Dad chimes in, "Let's all go sit in the living room and talk."

"I'm bringing the cookies," Syn adds and grabs a plate full.

"Have you been to see him?" I ask Aunt Brogan. She is holding my hand and mom has her arm around my shoulder.

"Yes, and I've been following his care closely. Captain Maynard has given me access to all his records. He was brought directly to the Portland base hospital and he has been seen by the best medical professionals in the military." She hesitates for a moment, seemingly trying to gather her thoughts.

"Physically, he will make a full recovery. He had some broken ribs that have long since healed and a few scars. Other than that, he'll be okay. He's getting the nutrition that he needs and physical therapy."

"What's the part you're not telling me?" I ask with a sob.

"Mentally, he will never be the same. He went through so much torment for so long that his chances of recovering are very slim. He won't even let anyone come in his room to cut his hair and beard. If they come near him with any instruments he withdraws on the floor into a ball. He refuses the medications that the doctors try to give him. He thinks they're trying to poison him."

I stand up, "I want to see him, today. I might be able to reach him."

"Sweetie, we will take you to him, but I don't want you to get your hopes up," Dad says as he meets me on my feet.

"There has to be something more they can do." I'm angry now.

"Please sit back down and I'll tell you the options." Aunt Brogan pulls at my hand.

I sit and demand, "Tell me."

"Obviously, they can give him more time," she frowns, "but I'm not sure that time is going to heal him. If they can get him to take his medication, the best we can hope for is that it will help him control his thoughts. It will also make him basically catatonic."

"That's a terrible plan," I interject.

"There's one other option, but you're not going to like it."

"You mean it gets worse?" I scowl at her.

"There is a very new sonogram procedure available for PTSD patients now. They can erase his memory from his time in the military and replace it with something good. They use ultrasound waves on the part of the brain that holds memory and they can place images in his head to replace the bad memories."

"That sounds like a good plan, not a bad one." I'm frowning at her.

Dad gets on the floor in front of me and takes both my hands in his lap. "Sweetie... he won't remember you," he says sadly.

"Why not, they can place images of me in his head...right?" I'm still frowning.

"It doesn't work that way. In order for him to heal, he cannot have anything left in his brain from the time he was in the military. They have to erase it all or it won't work," Aunt Brogan says with tears in her eyes.

"So, I'll be a new memory for him," I add hopefully.

58

"You won't be able to be in his life. The research has shown that anytime someone from the time that their memory was erased shows up, it negates their healing."

"Okay, you're right, that is a terrible option. I vote we give him more time, besides I'm his Power of Attorney and his Surrogate, the paperwork is in his military files, so they can't make any decisions without me."

"We will support whatever choice you make for him, but we don't want to see you hurt," Mom says.

"Let me go see for myself. Maybe I can help him."

The hour long ride to Portland seems eternal. Everyone insisted upon coming with me. Even Syn, who I tried to convince that he needed to rest after our ordeal.

The military hospital is state-of-the-art. Since the war with the Chinese, our government had to change things for military personnel. Being in the military is the highest paying job and our benefits far exceed all other plans. We are first in line for all new equipment and research.

Gone are the years of being treated like we were disposable, once we served. Our issues after that were ours to deal with. I've seen one too many PTSD soldiers over medicated to no longer be functional. I've also seen far too many commit suicide and destroy their families.

I was fortunate enough that therapy and small doses of medication helped me through my Post Traumatic Stress Disorder, not to mention my family support system. Crew has no family other than me and I need to figure out what will help him the most. I hate the idea of erasing his memory. Maybe that's selfish of me, but I'm just not ready to lose him again.

The hospital is eight stories high. Security is tight, but Captain Maynard meets us at the gate and escorts us through the building. It's bright and cheerful and everyone we pass has a smile on their face. It makes me feel better about him being here.

Aunt Brogan gets us through each door by scanning her badge. She takes us all the way to the seventh floor and greets the nurses at the station. She asks them to pull up his file. Inside, they should find the paperwork proving that I have all the rights to make all medical decisions for him. They quickly find it and give her permission to take me to his room. Everyone else goes to the waiting room to wait.

"Do you want me to go in with you? Aunt Brogan asks.

"No, I'll be fine. Are there security cameras in his room?"

"Yes, he has to be monitored at all times." Aunt Brogan gives me a hug, then heads back to the waiting room.

I blow out a huge breath to gather my composure, then I enter his room. It's not decorated. I notice all corners are rounded, no sharp edges. There's a bed, a table, and a television hanging on the wall. It's pretty basic and utilitarian. Aunt Brogan said there were cameras, but I don't see them. They must be well hidden.

I'm a soldier, I always check my surroundings first when I enter any unfamiliar location. I look into every corner of the room, mostly out of habit. It takes another moment for me to realize I don't see Crew anywhere.

"Crew," I call his name and hear a sound coming from another room. I cautiously walk around to where the sound came from and I see Crew standing in front of the bathroom mirror. He doesn't acknowledge me, he just stares into the mirror.

"It's me, Gray," I say softly. He blinks a few times but keeps his gaze locked in the mirror. He won't look at me.

He looks slightly heavier than the last time I saw him. But, he still doesn't resemble the powerful man that I remember. I walk behind his tall frame so that he can see my reflection. Maybe he just didn't recognize my voice?

"Do you remember me?" I quietly ask him.

"Yes," he says in his gravelly voice. It's changed somehow, I can't describe it. Aunt Brogan told me on the way here that his

60

vocal cords had been damaged by a long-term infection and that it will never sound the same.

I reach out to touch him and I see him flinch. "If you remember me, then you know I won't hurt you," I try to reassure him.

He turns to face me. He's wearing blue jeans and he's shirtless. I notice a comb in his hand. His hair is still a tangled mess. So is the wild beard he now has.

"That comb will never work for you."

"I want to cut my beard, but they won't give me a razor," he says.

"If you'll let me, I can shave it off for you."

He simply nods.

"Let me go get what I need and I'll be right back. Why don't you drag one of those chairs from the table in here so that you can sit down? It'll be easier for me because you're so tall."

He just nods again, this time more absently.

I press the button by the door to be let out. It occurs to me that he probably thinks he has traded one prison for another. He doesn't realize that at least this one is trying to help him and not hurt him. I walk into the waiting room and everyone stands up, waiting for me to speak.

"He has agreed to let me cut his beard," I say almost tearful. "He was just staring at his reflection in the mirror when I first saw him. I don't think he recognizes himself."

"I'll get you what you need." Aunt Brogan heads off to the nurse's station.

"That's progress, Sweetie. He hasn't let anyone else near him, according to the doctors," my mom says.

"It's a good sign," at least that's what I'm trying to tell myself. Aunt Brogan comes back with a basket full of toiletries that include a razor and scissors. She guides me back into his room.

Crew is sitting on the chair in the middle of the bathroom. I take out what I need and lay it on the counter. He's warily watching every move that I make. I pick up the scissors and a thick comb to help me get through his beard. I take a step forward and he grabs my hand that is holding the scissors. It startles me at first, then I see the look in his eyes. It's fear.

"I won't hurt you, I promise," I whisper, and he slowly releases my hand.

I cut through the thick strands of his beard slowly. His dark eyes remain fixed on mine.

"I have missed you so much," I whisper as the tears start to fall.

"Don't," he squeezes his eyes shut. "I can't bear to hear it, please." I see pain from his eyes to the corners of his lips.

"Okay," I'll give this to him for now. I don't want to push him too far, not this soon. He needs time.

I cut in silence until I make it to the point where I can shave him. I reach for the electric razor and show it to him. He nods and I continue to work on removing his beard. I see the dimple in his chin and it makes me smile. I always loved his face and this dimple gave him such character.

"What are you smiling about?" he asks cautiously.

"Your beautiful face, I finally found it under all this mess."

He doesn't respond, but he takes his hand and rubs it all over his face like he is trying to remember it too. He stands up and looks in the mirror and I could swear I see his eyes start to water.

"Will you cut my hair, too?" he asks, looking back at me in the mirror.

"Sure, I will." I smile at him, but he doesn't return it. "How short do you want it?"

"It doesn't matter, you decide." He sits back down.

I grab the brush and make a couple attempts to brush through it, but it's impossible. "This may be easier if it's wet."

He abruptly stands up and sheds his jeans and stalks into the shower. There is no door or curtain, it's an open shower. I watch him as he washes his hair. There are several scars that mar his back. His once firm muscular body is too frail, but I still see the beauty in him.

I want to dry him off so badly. Instead, I hand him a towel. He quickly dries and wraps his long hair into it. He pulls his jeans back on and sits down. I unwrap the towel and start slowly drying his hair. His eyes are closed, but his facial expression seems a little more relaxed. I try not to take too long in case he changes his mind. Some of the knots in his hair I'm unable to brush through so I take the scissors with his hair outstretched and cut them out. I decide not to cut it too short. I don't think a military haircut would be good for him right now. I cut it to the base of his neck. I never realized, he had curls in his hair. I had only known him to have a flat-top style cut. His brown curls are beautiful.

"There...all done." I move out of his view so that he can look in the mirror.

He stands up brushing the long strands of hair off of him. He runs his hands through his hair a few times. "Thank you for doing that." I see a small smile on his lips, but it doesn't reach the rest of his face.

"It was my pleasure. Is there anything else I can do for you?"

"Yes." He leans his long frame against the counter.

"You name it." I'm excited at the prospect of him letting me help him.

"You can leave now. PLEASE."

"What? But I thought..."

"I don't need any reminders of what I lost. I don't want to relive one minute of my time in something worse than hell. I didn't survive. The moment you were gone—I died. I didn't care what they did to me after that. I tried to kill myself multiple times, but they wouldn't allow it. They preferred tormenting their prisoner or having the pleasure of killing them themselves. I'm not the man you remember and I never will be."

"Not now, but maybe in time," I start hopefully.

"No, never," he states flatly. "The man you knew is gone. There is not an ounce of love or compassion in me for another living soul. Not ever again. Trust me, I'm completely empty." He stands with his arms crossed over his chest.

"Maybe you have had enough for one day? I'll come by again tomorrow," I say with tears starting to form again.

"Don't bother. I'll have your name removed from my visitor's list," he threatens harshly.

I feel like I've been slapped in the face. "I just want to help you," I say with a sob.

"I don't need or want your help, now leave me alone." He points to the door for me to leave.

I gather up the scissors and the razor and race past him. I stop with my finger on the button. "I love you, Crew," I say and push the button.

I make it to just outside the door and as soon as the door closes, as soon as he can no longer see me, I fall to my knees.

I lose all track of time. I have no idea how long I sat there defeated. Later, I feel my family surround me and pull me to my feet. I collapse again and Syn cradles me in his arms. I feel the movements of his steps as I bury my face in his neck. I hear the sound of my family's voices, but I can't make out what they're saying. My mind is screaming in pain.

The last thing I remember is Syn laying me down in the backseat of the Jeep and my head falling into my dad's lap.

CHAPTER

S teel and Ady made it home a few weeks ago and insisted that I stay with them. The rest of my family flew back home. Syn went with them but promised to be back in a few weeks. My mom and dad check in with me every day. Aunt Brogan keeps up with Crew's medical condition.

Crew has gotten more hostile and has quit eating. I think he just wants to die. The doctors are pushing me for a decision. They insist that things for him will only deteriorate if they don't treat him. I have slipped into a depression and stay in my room most of the time. I can't seem to make myself eat much. When I do go out, I go to the lighthouse and slip out onto the ledge where Ady once jumped to save her life and where she and Steel spent their wedding night beneath it.

I find myself sitting out here today, looking over the vast blue ocean. Even in daylight, I see the sweep of the light going across the water. I turn as I hear footsteps.

"Hey, Gray. I have someone I want you to meet," Ady says with Steel on her heels.

A beautiful brown lab comes up from behind them wagging his tail. He runs up to me and calmly sits beside me. He sniffs my face and then proceeds to lick me. I can't help but laugh.

"Who do we have here?" I ask between doggie licks.

"This is, Cy. He's a service dog. He's been trained to help people with PTSD and depression," Steel says.

"He's an emotional support dog," I clarify.

Ady sits down beside me. "Is this okay? We were trying to think of something that would help and we know how much you love our dogs."

Cy lays down and places his head on my lap and looks up at me with his big brown eyes. I can't help but like him. "It's fine. Thank you for wanting to help me, and putting up with me for the last several weeks. I'm sure it is not how you wanted to spend your time as newlyweds."

"Don't be silly, you're our family," Steel says as he sits down beside the dog and rubs his belly.

"Thank you both. I know I haven't been very good company moping around here."

"We've been trying to give you time and space, but mom says it's time to make a decision. Crew is acting out more and more, he is wasting away," Steel says as kindly as possible.

"I know. How does the procedure work?" I can hear the sadness in my voice. It feels like I have given up, but I remind myself this is giving him a fighting chance.

"From what I gather from mom, they will have to forcefully sedate him. After that, the process is simple." He reaches and takes my hand in his.

"What then?"

"They've laid out a plan to plant a memory of him being a private detective, it will allow him to use skills that he already has."

"Where will he live?"

"Here in Portland, so they can keep an eye on his progress."

"Can I see him before they erase his memory?"

"I don't think that's a good idea, for either one of you."

Cy must sense my distress because he curls further into my lap.

"There's one other thing," Ady says.

"What?" I look between the two of them, hoping it can't get any worse.

"Syn is going to be part of his life," Steel adds with a frown on his face.

"What do you mean?"

Since Crew didn't know Syn during his time in the military, they've chosen him to be his handler. Actually, Syn volunteered for it. He thought it might make you feel better if you knew he was being watched by someone you loved. He'll be in a partnership with him in the private security system business. Crew will probably do all the hard detective work and Syn will probably just sit with his feet propped on a desk," he laughs.

"Will I ever get to be in any part of his life?"

"No sweetie, only with what Syn shares with you," Ady says.

"I don't like any of it, but I guess I don't have a choice. I lost him once and survived, I guess I can do it again, if it means he will have a life."

"Unfortunately, I think it's his only hope." Steel scoots over and he and Ady both hug me.

"Okay. Tell Aunt Brogan to make the call." I cry in their arms and decide this will be the last time I cry over him. I have to let him go. "Thank you for Cy, too. It means a lot to me."

"We love you honey and want to do whatever we can to help you through this," Ady says crying along with me. Steel even has tears behind his eyes.

"I have a surprise for you," he says as he pulls me off the ground.

"I don't think I can handle any more surprises today," I sniff.

"You'll love this one, I promise," Ady says smiling.

"Lead the way."

We make it outside and they walk me to an area near Steel's gym, then they stop.

I look around the area and shield my eyes from the sun. "What is it that I'm looking for?" I ask them.

"We're going to build you your own container home, right here," he says while pointing to the ground.

"We want you to stay with us," Ady adds.

"You guys…"

"It's already a done deal, the containers come in tomorrow," Steel interrupts.

"I don't even know what to say…" A sob catches in my throat.

"Say you'll stay. I even have plans to add an outpost area for your parents."

"I love you both so much. Thank you." I hug them to me and Cy tries to stand in between us. I reach down and pat his head. "And thank you for him."

Over the next several weeks, I try to concentrate on the specifics of my new home being built. Steel has let me be part of the whole process. It has kept my mind away from what was being done to Crew's life. As long as I'm busy, I'm okay. Night time is the hardest. I wake up in a cold sweat and find Cy lying beside me nudging me with his wet nose. I think he wakes me when my dreams become more than I can handle.

I've single-handedly taken on the task of painting the exterior of the containers a deep red color. I like the physical work. Ady is better at the interior decorating than I am. She runs things by me, but ultimately I let her make the decisions.

I see a familiar Jeep pull into the driveway. I haven't seen Syn since that day in the hospital when he carried me out. Now, here he is in the flesh. I've really missed him but needed some distance. I'm sure he has to be concerned about how I feel with him being involved with Crew when I can't.

He walks slowly over to me. "Hey, sweetheart."

I freely walk into his outstretched arms, getting red paint on his white shirt.

He doesn't even mention it. "This place looks good."

"Steel and Ady have put a lot of work into making it a home for me."

"Give me a tour of the inside while we catch up."

The double-wide container is setup like a studio home, except I have a loft bedroom upstairs. There is a big brown leather couch that takes up most of the living room.

"Can I fix you a drink?" I ask him.

"Water would be good, thanks."

He follows me to the kitchen and sits down at the bar attached to the counter, and runs his hand across the top of it. "Is this concrete?"

"Yeah, Steel built it for me and Ady painted it black. I love it."

"They make a pretty good team," he says.

Sadness pulls at me. I would love for Crew and me to have had the chance to be a team again.

He senses it. "I'm sorry, sweetheart."

I hand him a glass of ice water. "It's okay. How is he?" I sit across from him at the bar and Cy gathers at my feet.

"He's doing okay. He's been eating and working out at the gym. He already looks so much better. The man is a machine in the gym. It won't be long and he will be back to his normal weight."

"What does he think happened to him causing him to be so thin?"

"He thinks he was really sick. Well, that's the story we built for him anyway."

"He really doesn't remember anything?" Cy's head is rubbing my leg.

"Not as far as I can tell. We opened the new office in Portland two days ago and we already have some business coming in."

"Where is he living?"

"We had him placed in an apartment downtown." He finally takes a drink of his water.

"Thank you for doing all this for him. I know at first I was angry that you get to be a part of his life and I don't." I reach across the bar and touch his arm.

"I did this for you, not Kell."

I'm quiet for a minute.

"He doesn't go by Crew. That was his military name, so it's important that he be called Kell."

I hop off the barstool and grab a beer out of the fridge. "I guess it doesn't really matter what he's called, I won't be calling him anything," I say a little harshly and Cy jumps on me. "It's okay, Cy. I'm okay." I pat his head and direct him back on the floor.

"I'm sorry. If it's easier for you, then we don't have to talk about him."

"Maybe in time... Right now, it's still too close to the surface. I want to know about you and how you're doing. I don't want this to come in between us."

He gets up and walks over to me, "We won't let it. You tell me when you want to hear more. I want to know that you're okay."

I hug him. "I will be, I promise."

CHAPTER 8

I can't believe I've lived in this house for almost an entire year now. I've gone back to school to get my nursing degree. I had taken some of my classes a few years ago but got side tracked on active duty. Thank God I did because I finished in a short amount of time. I've been working on an "as needed" basis in a hospital about twenty miles from here. The rest of my time, I volunteer to train service dogs like Cy. It has become my therapy.

With some pushing from Ady, I've decided it's time to get back into the real world and start dating. I dislike online dating, even if it's the best way to meet someone, it seems too impersonal. I was about to give up, then I found a place that still has old fashion speed dating. Ady was so excited that I decided to try it, that we went shopping for a dress. I can't remember the last time I wore a dress, but the shopping trip was fun.

"After your speed dating tonight, don't forget we're meeting up with Syn in Portland for a late dinner," she reminds me, as she styles my hair. "I want you to remember to have some fun tonight."

"I'll try, but I'm not hoping for much." Really, I'm just appeasing her.

I don't think I've ever been on a real date. Crew...I mean Kell and me never dated. We hit it off from the beginning. Syn updates me every now and then on him, but never gives a lot of details.

Syn says that the business is going great. I'm glad that they're busy and that it has all worked out for them. I don't think there was any other way he was going to give up the military.

I look in the mirror and I don't recognize myself. I have eyeshadow on and my brunette hair is straight and shiny, usually, it's unmanageable and I throw it in a ponytail or a braid. "Wow, you do great work." I smack my lips together, spreading my pink lipstick.

Steel walks in at that moment. "What have you done with my cousin? Who is that woman sitting there?" He teases his wife.

I backhand wave my hand at him as I watch him in the mirror.

"You look smoking hot, Cuz." He grins back at me.

"Ewe, I'm not sure that sounds right coming from you," I tease back. He shrugs his shoulders at me. "I'm not sure I'd call myself smoking hot."

"You look beautiful," Ady argues.

I stand and fidget in my dress that seems way too short.

"Good God, Girl! You have some sexy ass legs. Who knew?" Ady laughs. "I'm totally jealous."

Steel draws his wife into his side. "You can wrap you're sexy as sin legs around me anytime."

"On that note, I'm out of here. Sounds like you two need some alone time," I groan as I run for the door.

"Don't forget dinner tonight at nine!" Steel yells after me.

"Got it!" I yell back.

Speed dating was hilarious. I can't tell you how many new pick-up lines I learned. My ribs hurt from laughing so much. I didn't meet anyone that I was interested in, but it got me out of the house. I found myself comparing all of the men to Kell. None of them were even close to ever compete against him. There was zero connection to any of them.

It's only a short drive to the restaurant. I'm excited about seeing Syn. It's been several months since he and I connected. We talk on our links every few weeks. I know Kell's link had been destroyed when he was a prisoner, but I know he has since had it replaced. It's really strange that he doesn't remember any of it. I wish I had no memory of him. Actually, that's not true. I always want to remember being loved by him. Maybe one day I'll find someone that I can love again.

The restaurant is downtown Portland and it's huge. The valet takes my car and Syn greets me at the hostess counter.

"Hey, sweetheart! It's so good to see you." He hugs me close to him.

I draw back from him. "You, too."

He lets out a loud whistle that can be heard over the noise of the restaurant. "Don't you look nice?"

I turn beat red at the scene he makes and I grab his arm. "Come on and take me to the table."

"Steel and Ady are already here. He said they have an announcement to make."

"Well, let's go join them."

We all greet one another. I take a seat by Ady. "You look beautiful," I tell her.

"Thanks."

There is champagne chilling next to Steel. "What's the occasion?" I ask him.

"Let me pour some glasses and then we'll toast." He pours everyone but Ady a glass.

"Ady and I are pregnant...well, Ady is pregnant, but I had some part in it." He is beaming from ear to ear.

"Oh my God, congratulations!" I hug Ady.

"It sure took you long enough," Syn ribs Steel.

"Not even you can piss me off tonight, brother." He raises his glass for a toast and we all clink our glasses together.

"Do Aunt Brogan and Uncle Kyren know yet?" I ask.

"We called them on the way here. I think they're planning on invading our fortress," he's still smiling.

"I really am so happy for the two of you. You guys deserve happiness. When are you due?"

"Six months from now. February fourteenth, to be exact."

"A Valentine's baby!" We all toast again.

We order our food and we're all caught up in laughter when I look up and see someone standing in the distance behind Syn.

It's not just anyone. It's Kell Crew. I fight back my gasp of astonishment, but my heart had to have skipped a beat.

He has his hand at the small of the back of a drop-dead gorgeous redhead.He's smiling and looks good now, he looks almost the exact way I remember him when we were happy together. My mouth must have been hanging open and my gaze fixed. All eyes turn to where mine are. I can't breathe. Of course, he found someone else. I can't help but feel a little bitterness, even jealousy toward that lucky woman with him.

He isn't supposed to see me. Not ever. He's looking over at us and waving.

And now, he's walking right up to our table. He's partners with Syn, so Crew will be friendly with him in public. How did none of us foresee this possibility? I can't breathe. I don't think I can do this.

"Hey, Syn. Fancy seeing you here," he says as Syn stands and shakes his hand. My cousin tries to direct him away from our table. I overhear him say that Crew was supposed to be out of town. I continue to ease drop on his answer that his plans got changed at the last minute. Then, he has the nerve to smile at the redhead that I believe has horns growing out of her head.

"What are you doing here?" he asks Syn.

"I'm having dinner with my family." Stress is written all over Syn's face.

"Well, I would love to meet them." He turns toward our table and Syn keeps a strong arm on his shoulder.

He introduces Steel and Ady first. I want to crawl under the table and hide. His eyes meet mine and I could swear there is a connection. He sticks his hand out for me to shake and I feel electricity going through it. His smile changes to a frown.

"Do I know you?" he asks with a puzzled look.

I have to get out of here. "No, I don't believe we've met," I say as I get up from the table. "If you all will excuse me, I'm not feeling very well." No one tries to stop me. They're as shocked as I am.

I run past him and barely make it into the ladies room before I hurl in a toilet. I'm still retching when I hear the sound of Ady's voice outside the stall. She must have followed right behind me.

"Gray, are you okay?" she asks in a worried voice.

I open the stall door after I crawl off the floor. I move to the sink to splash water on my face. There are no tears. Thank God there is no one else in here but Ady and me.

"I'm so sorry that happened," she says rubbing my arm.

Why did he have to look so damn good? He was dressed in a suit and even under it, I could tell that he had bulked back up. He left his hair a little longer like the day that I'd cut it. No beard and that damn dimple was staring me in the face.

After all this time, I knew I still loved him the moment our eyes connected a minute ago. I could live with that, but I couldn't live with the thought of messing things up for him by seeing me. However, I did want to kill that woman. Because her being there, meant that he had moved on and I had not. She is why he is still in town, he'd said. This is all her fault.

"I'll be fine. Just give me a minute, please."

"Okay," she says sweetly. "We're all here if you need us."

"This is you and your husband's night. I'm not going to let this ruin it."

I take the time to pee and rinse my mouth out a few times. I can do this, that's what I keep telling myself anyway. I straighten my hair and check my dress one last time and exit the bathroom. As I do, I look up and Crew is leaning against the wall with his long legs crossed at the ankles.

Now what? How the hell am I going to get by him? What's he doing standing there? He looks up and sees me before I can dart back into the restroom. He pulls himself upright before approaching me.

"Are you okay?" he asks me in that gravelly voice.

"I'm fine," I say, trying to be short with him and move past him.

His hand reaches out and takes my elbow. "Did I say something that upset you? You look really upset. Are you sure we've never met?"

He has no idea. This isn't his fault. Nor is it fair to risk his newfound happiness with my presence.

"You just remind me of someone I once knew, that's all." I try not to look into the pool of his brown eyes.

"You vaguely remind me of someone, too."

I wish MY memory was vague. "I'm sure it's a coincidence." I continue past him, back to our table. He doesn't follow me.

Syn stands and holds my chair out for me. "I'm so sorry, I thought he was out of town. I've never seen him here before anyway, I thought we were safe. We can leave now if you want to."

"It's okay, I'm fine. Let's just try to appear normal, if he comes back. I want us to finish our meal together and celebrate the new baby." I take the bottle of champagne and pour myself another glass. I guzzle it down and quickly pour myself another.

I can't help but look around, part of it is my training kicking in during stressful situations. I want to know where he is, then I spot him at a faraway table with his date.

I'm so grateful they weren't seated near us. I can't stand to watch him with another woman. I've never been so jealous of anyone in my life. She has the life that I want. The man that I want. The future that I DESERVED. Damn it, maybe I should've taken that speed dating thing more seriously. I have got to get over him once and for all.

We finish our meal and I feel bad that the excitement over a new baby got overrun by me seeing him again. I try to make things better. "Can I help you decorate the baby's room?" I ask Ady.

"I'd love that. Thank you. I can't be around paint fumes without being sick."

"I've probably thrown up enough tonight for the both of us," I joke quietly.

I know she is appeasing me. Because I've already proven that I have no decorating skills, otherwise I would've decorated my own home.

"Are you going to find out the sex of the baby?"

"I want to, but Steel wants it to be a surprise." She smiles over at him.

"He's old-fashioned in some ways," I add.

"You mean he is a grumpy old man," Syn says laughing.

"And you, dear brother, are a pain in my ass," Steel ribs back.

"You're going to have to learn to watch your potty mouth, Mister," Ady pokes her finger in Steel's chest.

I see him snuggle up to her. "If I remember correctly, you were the one always in trouble for using bad language." She smiles and kisses him, obviously a shared memory between them.

"Are you two ever going to quit acting like newlyweds?" Syn asks, sarcastically.

"I hope not," is Steel's response as he sweetly kisses his bride.

"Haven't you ever been in love, Syn?" I ask him.

"Not even remotely close," he laughs.

77

"One day you're going to meet a woman that captures your heart and soul."

"There is only one thing I want a woman to capture and it's not my heart, sweetheart."

"You're so gross." I laugh at him.

"Okay, you two. It's time to pay the bill and head home."

I get my keys from the valet who brought up my car and Syn opens my door. "It really was good to see you tonight," I tell him.

"It was. And again, I'm so sorry about Kell tonight."

"You two really are friends, aren't you?"

"Yeah, he's a really good guy. I wish the two of you could be together," he says sadly.

"This coming from 'Mister Romantic,'" I tease him, to keep from getting too emotional over his comment.

"I'll see you in a couple of weeks. Steel and I have a fishing trip planned."

Portland is beautiful at night. Instead of taking the highway, I decide to drive through the city and maybe sneak a peek at Syn's office. I speak the name of the company and my Jeep's navigation system pulls it up. It's only five minutes from here.

I drive slow as I come up to the building. My breath hitches as I see Crew unlocking the door. My heart stops.

I sit at the red light staring at him. He goes inside and disappears until I see a light come on in the apartment upstairs. I didn't realize he lived here.

A horn blows behind me and gets my attention. I'm sitting through a green light. I slowly drive by and it takes everything in me to not stop. I'm thankful that I didn't see that wretched redhead walk in with him. I might've run her over with my Jeep. That may have looked a little suspicious on my part.

The rest of the ride home, my mind keeps flashing back to moments I had with him. I used to love watching him put on his uniform in the mornings after he crawled out of my bed. I was always blessed with the sight of his fine ass. The way he carried himself, kind of like tonight, was such a turn on for me. I would watch him shave and end up with the shaving cream on my face because I couldn't resist kissing him. We would wind up on the floor tangled around one another. What I miss the most, was making him laugh. He had such a great laugh and a sexy smile.

I have got to stop this. Seeing him tonight doesn't change my reality. I will never have him again. Maybe I'll try the speed dating again. For now, I just want to go home and curl up in my bed. I'm sure Cy is going to be all over me tonight, sensing my whirlwind of emotions.

CHAPTER
9

I finally got around to going speed dating again and I actually met someone that was really nice. His name is Max. He's a computer programmer. His job sounds kind of boring, but he seems really sweet.

I'm meeting Max tonight at a diner outside of Portland. I didn't tell anyone because I didn't want them to make a big deal out of it. They've been treating me with kid gloves for over a month now, ever since my unexpected run in with Crew.

I see Max is already seated at the table when I arrive. He stands to greet me and pulls out a chair for me. "You look pretty," he says before he kisses my cheek.

"Thank you. You look nice, too." He really does. He's wearing a navy sports jacket and slacks.

Our conversation seems easy as we drink our wine and finish up our food. He's telling me something about computer software I don't have any clue about. Then I hear my name spoken in my link.

"Excuse me for a minute," I say as I get up. Max is such a gentleman, he stands.

"I'll be right back." I step outside so that I can hear better than inside the busy restaurant.

"Hello."

"Is this Gray?"

I recognize his voice immediately. That gravelly sound is unforgettable.

"Cr...I mean Kell?" My heart is pounding. Why is he calling me?

"I haven't been able to get you out of my head since the night I met you. I know that's strange, but I had to talk to you."

What could be the harm in talking to him? He can't see my face. "What is it you want from me?" I ask almost in a whisper like other people could hear my conversation.

"I...I just wanted to say hi." He sounds nervous.

"Hi." I can't believe I'm talking to him. My heart feels like it's going to explode.

"Can I see you?"

I want to say yes so badly. "I don't think that's a good idea. You work with my cousin." I know it's a lame excuse but it's the only thing I could come up with on the spur of the moment.

"Well, what if I okay it with Syn?" he asks.

God, he is not making this easy. "Actually, I'm seeing someone. I'm on a date right now." I want to cut my heart out of my chest.

"I'm sorry to interrupt, but can I link with you again at another time?"

I forgot that he doesn't take no for an answer. My excuse would have stopped any other man.

"Another time. Yes." I end our link and bend over to try and suck air into my lungs. Why did I tell him that? Maybe part of me doesn't think it could hurt to talk to him, the other part physically aches to hear his voice.

I regain my physical composure, but I can feel my heart remains racing as I return to my date.

My heart isn't in it now. I half listen to what Max is saying, while my mind drifts to Kell.

I need to try to focus. Kell is not a possibility, the man in front of me is. He's handsome, even though I've never been attracted to blonde men. He's lean with a few muscles. They're not bulging like Kell's.

Gah...get it together, Gray. I force myself to be in the conversation as we finish our meal.

He holds the door open for me and walks me to my car. "I would love to take you out again," he says with a sweet smile.

"That would be nice."

He starts to lean in to kiss me and I give him my cheek. I can't do this. I can't lead him on. "Max, dinner was great and you're really sweet, but...I'm just getting over someone and I think it's too soon. I'm so sorry." I felt guilty, but it wasn't a lie. I am trying to get over someone I can never have again.

"Oh," he shuffles his feet, "I understand. When and if you decide you're ready, you know how to reach me." He opens my car door and I quickly get inside. "Thanks again for dinner." He waves and shuts the door.

I feel so bad. I can't compare every guy to Kell. Sometimes I think he really did ruin me for other men, just like he boasted he would when we had sex for the first time.

The car drive home is lonely. I hear my link click in and for a moment I hope that it's him again.

"Hey, Sweetheart. Where are you?" It's Syn's voice is in my ear now.

"I went on a date." I feign excitement.

"Really? It must not have been very good if he didn't take you back home with him." He laughs.

"Not every date leads to sex, Syn." I scold him.

"Well, it should." He laughs again.

"You're not right, you know that? Why aren't you out on a date on a Saturday night?"

"We've been a little busy at work. Someone keeps stealing some expensive art from one of our clients. We haven't been able

to get a lead on whoever it is and our client is furious. So, I've been working a little overtime."

"Ah, poor Syn," I mock him.

"I need to tell you something." His voice sounds so serious all of a sudden.

"What?"

"Kell has been asking a lot about you. I wanted to give you a heads up in case he tries to link up with you."

"Has he?" I don't want him to know that he already linked with me. I know I am lying by not telling Syn. And why hadn't he warned me sooner?

"He has been like a dog with a bone since the night he saw you in the restaurant."

"Do you think he suspects anything?" I'm curious.

"No, I just think the man has a hard-on for you."

"Nice way to put it, Syn." I scold him again.

"Look, I don't want you to get hurt. If he links to you, please don't answer him and let me know right away. I'll make up some excuse."

"Okay." I lie to Syn for the second time tonight. At least I was honest with Max.

"Try harder on the date next time," he laughs as he disconnects.

Cy is all over me when I get home. I know I train dogs, but I still don't understand how they sense different emotions from fear, depression, and anger, just to mention a few. He does his job and calms me right down. I curl up with him in the bed. He's such a bed hog. By the middle of the night, I will only have a small corner.

I dream of a tall, dark, handsome man in a military suit and I wake up sad again. You would think by now my mind would find something else to dream about. I give up on sleep and take a long hot soothing shower.

I delve into my work at the hospital for a few days and it brightens my mood. I love helping people and it's quite the contrast from being a sniper.

Ady has asked me to go maternity shopping with her. I think Steel drew the line on shopping. Her belly barely has a round bump, but Steel can't keep his hands off of it. He is going to be such a great dad. Who would have thought over a year ago that he would be so happy and having a baby?

"Do you have any more dates lined up?" Ady asks as she scrolls through the racks.

"No, the last one didn't go so well. There is this guy at the dog training facility that I think kind of likes me." I add.

"Really?" She sounds way too excited. "What does he look like?"

"He's about my height, with muscular, tattooed arms."

"Sounds nice." She enters the dressing room and I sit outside the door.

"Has he asked you out?"

"Not exactly. He wanted to know if I wanted to have coffee one night when we were leaving work."

"Did you go with him?"

"No."

"Why not? I swear you are your own worst enemy." She peeks her head out.

"I know, I know. Next time I'll say yes."

"You need to ask him this time... You probably scared him off." She steps out in a cute little maternity dress.

"Steel will love that! It shows off your legs. Then again, you could walk around in a potato sack, and he would still find you sexy as hell."

She smiles, "I know. He would, wouldn't he? I'm so lucky to have him."

"I think HE'S the lucky one. He wasn't even that nice until you came back into his life."

"We're good for each other."

"Did I ever tell you that I can't have children?" I don't know why I picked this moment to share this with her. I already kind of regret it. I finally had to tell someone.

She gasps, "No!" Before she sits down beside me.

"I was pregnant with Kell's baby when they threw us in those cages. One of the Chinese soldiers kicked me in the stomach. I miscarried and their bastard of a doctor took everything out of me."

"Oh, Sweetie! I'm so sorry."

"Kell never knew that I was pregnant."

"That must have been so hard for you to go through alone."

"I didn't tell him because I just knew he would try to kill them and he would've gotten himself killed."

"And you feel like maybe you should've let him know and then he wouldn't have suffered all those years."

She read my mind. "Yes, and I've never admitted that out loud," I add sadly.

"You have to forgive yourself for anything that happened back then. Nothing was in your control. You made decisions based on survival, you had no idea what the outcome was going to be." She hugs me.

"I know you're right and it's time for me to really let Kell go. I think I'll take your advice and ask Adam out."

"Good, now let's finish shopping!" She hops up.

Piles of clothes later, we make it home. I quickly change before I leash up Cy and head to the dog training facility.

Adam is in the middle of working with a dog when he sees me. He waves and continues his session.

I go check on the motley crew in the back and make sure they all have fresh water and food. I pat their heads as the come up to me. These dogs have become my second family and Cy enjoys his visits with them. "Go play," I tell him as I let him loose in the yard.

I work my session, training two German Shepherds while waiting for Adam to finish up. "Nice work with that Pit Bull today," I say making conversation.

"He has come a long way." He smiles at me.

"So... can I take you up on that cup of coffee after work?" I ask shyly.

"Yes, I would love that," he says with a big smile suddenly splitting his face.

The door chimes as someone enters. I turn to greet whoever it is and gasp.

Oh my God! It's Kell Crew in a pair of tight ass jeans and a black t-shirt that hugs every muscle on his chest and abs. I'm in shock and my mouth hangs wide open. Adam looks at me and frowns before walking up to Kell with his hand held out.

"Can I help you?" he asks him.

"Actually, I'm here to see Gray about a service dog." He passes by Adam and stands directly in front of me.

"How did you know where I work or that I would even be here?"

"I'd like to say I am a really good detective, which I am. I simply searched your name on the internet. I took a chance that you would be here." He shrugs his shoulders at me.

Adam walks up and looks concerned. "Is there a problem here, Gray?" He looks at him and then at me.

"No, not at all. I'll show him the facility and some of the dogs."

"Are we still on for coffee?" he asks.

Now it's my turn to look back and forth between the two of them. "Yes...just let me finish up here and I'll meet you at the coffee house on the corner." Kell doesn't look too happy.

"I'll see you there," Adam says as he leaves.

"Hi," Kell says with a smile.

"Why are you really here?" I stand with my hands on my hips.

"I wanted to see you and I didn't want to take no for an answer."

"I told you that I don't think this is a very good idea. My cousin doesn't like his employees involved with his family."

He takes a step closer and I can smell his aftershave. I can feel my heart drumming wildly in my chest. "Your cousin...does not control me," he rasps.

Oh my God, oh my God—if he comes one step closer I'm not going to be able to control myself. I take a step back. "What is it that you want from me?"

"I want to get to know you. I've felt a connection to you the moment I laid eyes on you in the restaurant."

"You mean you were able to take your eyes off the redhead you were with," I say with a little venom.

His turn to take a step back. "She was just a friend."

Jealousy takes over. "Does she know that? Because she couldn't take her eyes off of you." Damn it, I need to shut up. She's really not my enemy, I don't know her. Kell deserves to be happy.

He steps closer again. "I'm glad that you were paying such close attention." He reaches out and brushes his hand down my arm.

"I don't like a man that would notice another woman while he was out on a date."

"It wasn't a date, I told you that. And any man would have to be blind not to notice you."

I swallow hard and back away from his touch when all I really want to do is run into his arms. "You need to leave." I manage to breathe out.

Instead of getting mad, he smiles. Oh, no. I'm done for, this is how he won me over the first time.

What the hell am I going to do to get rid of him? All I really want to do is keep him here with me.

"I'm dating Adam."

I just ripped my own guts out, threw them on the floor, and then I stomped on them just to make sure I felt enough pain.

"Him?" he points to the door.

"Yes, him." I stand firm.

"He's not your type." He smiles bigger.

"How would you know what my type is?" I scowl at him.

"I'm your type, you just don't know it yet." He says it as he backs his way to the door. "I'll see you again very soon, Gray." He winks at me and leaves.

I shakily find the keys to lock up and head over to the coffee shop where Adam has found us a table by the big glass windows. He smiles as soon as he sees me.

"Hey," I say as I slide into the seat across from him. "Sorry, I'm late. I had to let someone know about leaving Cy there."

He doesn't look convinced. "You okay?" he frowns.

"Yea, I'm fine." I plaster on a fake smile. Thank God, the waitress walks up to our table to take our order. It gives me a minute to try and focus on the man in front of me.

"I'll have a Vanilla Chai Tea Latte." Adam gives his order and then there is a moment of awkward silence.

"I like your tattoos." I had to say something to break the ice.

"Thanks." He rolls up his t-shirt sleeve, exposing his shoulder. "They all have a meaning."

As Adam is telling me what each one represents, I hear that gravelly voice.

"You look beautiful." I don't say anything back, but I scan the café. I don't see him, but I hear his laughter. I glance out the window and I see him sitting in a doorway across the street. He sees me the minute I find him and he waves. *"Here I am, baby."*

It's Kell. He's actually in my head. I'm hearing him over my link.

"Stop." My interruption startles me as much as Adam.

Adam stops mid-sentence. "What?"

"I...I missed what you said about the cross tattoo meant to you." Oh my God, I literally have to get him out of my head. He can't have tapped into my link with spyware, could he? He's a detective now, I remind myself.

Adam starts talking again and I try to focus solely on him.

"It won't work, he's not the man for you." My head buzzes with his voice.

"What kind of things do you like to do when you're not at work, Adam?"

We'll see what kind of man he is. I've been told to try harder on dates. I really want to like Adam.

"I like to ride the dunes."

"Ha — kid's stuff. Not a real man." Kell laughs.

Kell heard Adam? Damn it, Kell does have spyware in his link so he can hear not only me but every word Adam says, too. I'll fix his ass.

"That sounds very exciting. I hope it isn't too dangerous. I have seen the dunes on the coast, but I have never ridden them."

Maybe my interest will shut Kell up. I take a sip of my coffee and wait.

"There is only one thing that you would be interested in riding with me." His sexy voice echoes in my ear and I choke on my coffee.

"Are you okay?" Adam sounds worried.

"Hot." I wave my hand in front of my face.

"Let me get you some water." He gets up and heads to the counter.

I cover my mouth, so no one sees me talking out loud to myself. "What the hell are you doing? Would you mind turning off your spy link?" I whisper between gritted teeth.

"I'm trying to distract you from the wrong man."

I look over in his direction and he shrugs his shoulders at me.

"I've already told you that you and I are not happening. Now, leave me alone!"

89

Adam returns to the table with my water. I reach across and touch his hand. "Thank you." I hear a fierce growl in my ear, it startles me and I jump.

"Are you sure you're okay? We can do this another time."

"I'm sorry, I'm just distracted, I keep replaying someone's conversation in my head and it has me a little shook up." It's like I want to shut it off, but I can't.

Kell laughs in my ear. *"Quick thinking, baby."*

"Anything I can help with?" Adam asks.

He is so damn sweet.

"No, but thank you for offering. Can we do this another night? There is something I really need to go deal with."

"Yes, come deal with me," Kell agrees.

"Sure. I'm off for a couple of days. Maybe we could do dinner one night after work?"

"I would like that," I smile at him.

"No, you wouldn't," Kell growls.

"Thank you for being so understanding."

"Let me walk you out." Adam stands.

"Don't be silly, finish your coffee. I have to go back and get Cy. He's very protective, too. He won't let any strangers near me."

"He will let me, baby." Kell is still talking.

I exit the café and head straight toward the man that has my head swimming.

I turn my head back to check behind me, just to make sure Adam isn't watching. He's not, he's already distracted by his phone.

Kell gets up off his perch and stands to face me. I have to remind myself that I'm angry with him. I would rather be running into his arms than telling him to leave me alone. His tall muscular body makes my body come alive. I grab his hand to pull him out of sight but regret it the minute I do. I feel that pull to him again.

"Are you crazy?" Part of me regrets those words. He's not crazy. He was never supposed to see me. He'd been traumatized, this memory wipe made him better. He can't remember me, without remembering all of it, the good and the bad.

He smiles down at me. "I'm going crazy for you to say yes to a date with me."

"We have been over this already. You and I cannot date." I try to frown at him but he has a triumphant smile on his face. "And if you ever eavesdrop on my conversation again, I will kick your ass myself! I could have you arrested. Or tell my cousin you are harassing me. How many times do I have to tell you no?"

He pulls me to his firm warm body. "Name one part of your body that doesn't want you to say yes."

Holy hell. I squirm out of his embrace. "You are awfully sure of yourself."

"I'm just a man that knows what he wants and I'm willing to do anything to get it."

I know I'm going to hate myself later, but I can't help it.

"If I agree to go out with you, will you quit stalking me and not tell Syn about it? I mean it, one and only one date. And you cannot ever let Syn know. I'm serious. Promise me."

"Cross my heart." He leans in closer.

I place my hand on his chest and softly push him further away. "I agreed to a date nothing else. I need to go get my dog." I turn to walk away and he follows me.

"Your date should've never let you leave by yourself."

"I'm sure if he knew I was being stalked, he never would have."

"You can never be too careful. There are a lot of crazy people out here," he laughs.

"Tell me about it." I squint my eyes at him and he laughs again. I love the sound of his laughter. I've missed it so much.

I unlock the door and Cy greets me. Even more strangely, he runs past me and rubs all over Kell's legs.

Of course, he did. Why am I surprised?

"Traitor." As if Cy could understand me.

"See? Even your 'very protective dog', as you yourself put it, knows who's good for you." He pats him on the head. "Don't you, Boy?"

I lock back up and he walks Cy and me to the Jeep. "So, what about that date?"

"How about Saturday night?"

"Okay, I am going to hold you to it. Remember, I know how to get a hold of you if you try and stand me up." He laughs. "I'll connect with you Saturday morning with plans."

He shuts the door. I watch him watching me as I pull away.

"What the hell have I agreed to, Cy?"

Cy just looks at me and gives a happy bark.

CHAPTER

S leep totally escapes me. Thoughts of Kell keep racing through my mind. I'm thankful he hasn't tried to link with me again. I decide to make good use of my sleepless night and head to my desk downstairs to do a little research on my computer. Cy curls up at my feet.

"Research Ultrasound outcomes for PTSD patients." My computer pulls up pages of results. I spend the next several hours glued to the screen, reading everything I can to find results about memory wipe patients being reintroduced to someone from their past. In ninety-eight percent of the cases, over a one month time period, all of their memories came back making the treatment ineffective.

"Ninety-eight percent," I tell Cy, who is sleeping underneath me. I don't know how I can selfishly risk two percent. I don't know that Kell is going to let me stop him. Maybe I should tell Syn. My mind says yes, but my heart says no. I'm only human and I can only resist so much when my heart is aching. It says over a month, I could keep a good eye on him if he shows any signs of changes, then I could disappear from his life again. Just one date couldn't hurt.

I bury myself in work the rest of the week. I have nearly jumped out of my skin every time my link went off. I'm greeted by Syn at my door Friday afternoon.

"What are you doing here?" Surely Kell didn't tell him anything...

"Steel, Ady and I are headed up to McCall for our fishing trip."

"I had forgotten about that. I didn't realize that Ady was going, too?"

"Steel won't let her out of his sight. Besides, Ady loves the cabin. Do you want to join us?"

"No thanks. I have some work to do this weekend." Thank God, he doesn't know anything about my date with Kell. "How is Kell by the way?" I try to be nonchalant about my question.

"He seems happier this past week. He finally quit asking about you, so I think he has finally given that up."

"Oh...um, that's good."

"Sorry, you know I didn't mean it that way. And I know you've been dating some and trying to move on with your life and he needs to do the same."

I'm not very good at lying. "I had another date earlier this week," I blurt out.

"That's great! Anyone I know?"

"A guy I work with training dogs."

"So, how did it go?"

"It didn't end in sex if that is what you're asking me."

"That's not what I'm asking." He looks sincere.

"I felt like I was comparing him to Kell the entire time." If he only knew that Kell was on the date with me.

"He will be a hard man to measure up to, but you need to keep trying."

I want to tell him so badly, but I'm afraid he will move him so far away from me that I will never see him again. "I will." I'm really hating myself right about now.

I help them all load into the SUV. Steel's Pit Bulls climb in the very back. "Are you sure you don't want to leave them here with me, Ady?"

"They love to go with us. Besides, I want you to have a nice peaceful weekend. You'll have the entire fortress to yourself."

The place is so quiet without everyone here. I decide to take Cy down by the water to play with Artemis. I curl up on the blanket and watch the two of them splash around in the water. My thoughts—as usual, these days—go to Kell. I wonder what he has planned for us tomorrow? I wonder what he is doing right now?

My body heats up at the thought of him. I squeeze my legs together, but it doesn't dull the ache. He is the only man that I've had sex with. My body still belongs to him after all these years. I can't bear the thought of ever letting another man touch me like he has.

Adam is handsome and has a nice body, but I don't have any desire to have sex with him. Sometimes I think, I should just do it to see if it is just in my head that Kell owns my body. Thinking about him has me all hot and bothered.

I lay on my back and run my hand to the waist of my shorts. I slowly glide my hand inside. My panties are already wet. I slip my hand underneath them.

"*You were thinking about me weren't you?*" I hear in my link. I gasp and look around.

How the hell did he know? "No," I lie and sit up, "I'm on the beach with Cy."

He chuckles. "*I couldn't wait another day to talk to you. I have the whole day all planned out for tomorrow.*"

"The entire day? I only agreed to one date." I find myself smiling.

"*Who's to say how long a date can last. I need as long as I can get to convince you that I'm your type.*"

I don't need convincing that's for sure.

"Let's just take it one date at a time, for now."

"Who has hurt you so badly that you're so afraid to take a chance?" he asks with all sincerity.

You! YOU have...

"It was a guy a long time ago. It took me awhile to get over him," I say softly. "In fact, I'm not sure that I will ever be over him. How is that fair to you?"

"Give me a chance and I promise that you will fall in love with me."

I'm already in love with you... "Don't count on it." I love cocky Kell. "Details, I need details of where you are taking me.

"I'm going to pick you up at eleven. Except I don't know where you live."

I'm so thankful everyone is gone for the weekend. I give him my address.

"The rest is a surprise."

"That's not details. And I'm not big on surprises, either." I laugh at him.

"A guy can't give all his moves away, now can he?" I can hear him smile.

"Okay, Romeo. I'll see you tomorrow."

I'm truly surprised that he let me disconnect without a fight. I know I shouldn't, but I can't wait to spend time with him tomorrow. We never had a chance to date before, so maybe it won't bring back any memories for him.

I hear a noise off in the distance and Cy starts to bark. I get up and look around, but I don't see anything. I know Steel upgraded his security system after the ordeal with Ady. I decide to go check the computer system to see if it picked up anything.

I make the trek up the rocky cliff with Cy in tow. Steel left me a key to his house in case I needed anything. One of the monitors is flashing a warning. I scroll through the different camera areas, but I don't see anything too concerning. Whatever set it off moved quickly, probably an animal. I clear the alarm and reset it.

"Come on, Cy. Let's go back to the house and watch a movie. I'll make you some popcorn." He wags his tail and then follows me.

I didn't get much sleep through the night thinking about my day with Kell. I'm excited and worried at the same time. I take a long, hot shower. I give myself enough time to blow dry and straighten my hair. I'm not sure where he's taking me, so I'm torn between what to wear. After emptying out my closet, I pick a pair of white skinny jeans to go with my blue and white striped top that lays off the shoulders. I add a cute pair of navy sandals to the ensemble. I finish up as the gate alarm sounds.

"Kell, why didn't you just link with me to let me know you were close?"

"I didn't want to give you a chance to change your mind." He laughs

"Give me a minute to get the remote."

"Hurry up. I'm dying to see you."

He drives up in a sleek, black Hummer. Why am I not surprised? He parks and when he opens the door, I instantly start to throb. He has on the sexiest pair of faded blue jeans sitting low on his waist with an army green color t-shirt stretched across his chest.

"You look beautiful." He leans in and kisses my cheek.

"You...um...look pretty good there, yourself." Why am I stammering? I have seen this guy naked many times before. I have never been shy around him.

"This place is nice." He scans the area.

"This is Steel and Ady's fortress." I wave my hand in the air.

"You will have to give me a tour sometime, but we need to get going." He takes my elbow and leads me to the Hummer. He even opens the door for me. Who knew he could be such a gentlemen?

We head down the drive. "Where are we going? I wasn't sure what to wear?"

"You're perfect." He puts his hand on my thigh. "Where is your family this weekend?"

"Doesn't Syn tell you anything?"

"No, as a matter of fact, he doesn't. He's very tight-lipped when it comes to his family, especially you."

"Oh, they're not home. They all went fishing up at Steel's cabin."

He casts his eyes in my direction. "So, this means you have the fortress all to yourself?"

He makes that sexy as hell sound in his throat. "Me and Cy." I smile at him and he literally growls.

I need to change the subject. "How are you liking your job?"

"It's good. We're staying busy. Syn lets me handle the investigations and he handles the day to day stuff, but I think he misses being in the field."

"I have a hard time picturing him behind a desk and not in complete control."

"He's a good guy."

"He says the same thing about you."

"How is your dog training job going? Been out with any co-workers lately?" He winks at me.

"I figured with your stalking skills you would already have the answer to that." I laugh at him.

"I'm hoping to win you over, so you never want another man."

His words hit me hard. They take me back to the first time he said them to me. I fight back my emotions and stare out the window.

"You're awfully quiet. Did I say something to upset you?"

I reach over and touch his hand on the steering wheel. "No, I'm fine. It was just some old ghosts rearing their ugly heads."

For the rest of the drive, he tells me about some of the cases he is working on. I love to listen to him talk. I miss his old voice, but this one seems even sexier. We pull up to a dive of a restaurant that sits on the shoreline of the ocean. The name on the faded blue sign reads, Boondocks.

"Have you ever been here before?" he asks as we head through the pebbles that line the beach.

"No, but it looks like the kind of place I would really like." I smile at him and he takes my hand and leads the way up the wobbly stairs.

"They have the best fish sandwiches on the entire west coast."

"I bet it's freshly caught." I grasp my fingers around his hand. I love the feel of his touch mingled with mine.

He leads me to a table that overlooks the water. "This is such a great place. Why is there no one else here?" I ask as he pulls my chair out for me.

"I wanted you all to myself with no distractions." He sits beside me rather than across from me.

My mouth hangs open. "You rented the entire restaurant for the day?"

"No, actually just for lunch. I have other plans later."

I don't even know what to say to that. I have so many questions I want to ask him, but not here. "That was very sweet of you."

I see on him something I have never seen before, a small, shy smile. He is always so confident, it surprises me.

Our lunch conversation came so easily. At one time, he was telling me jokes. I got so caught up in laughter, I snorted. Then he proceeded to make fun of me for the next twenty minutes.

He was right, the food was delicious and I really enjoyed his company.

"Are you ready for what's next on the agenda?"

"Are you going to tell me what it is?"

"See that sailboat docked over there?" he points to a dock on the side of the restaurant.

"You're taking me sailing?"

His smile is so big and infectious. "Yes."

I would say this is a 40ft cruising sailboat. It looks like it is an older boat that has been refurbished. The seats around the table are covered in white and the stairs leading to the cabin are right behind them.

I have been on all kinds of boats, but I have never been sailing. "Do you even know how to sail?" I ask, grinning at him.

"No, but I hired a captain so that I could spend all my time sweeping you off your feet."

"Well, I'd say you are off to a pretty good start."

He pulls me out of my chair and places a soft kiss on my lips. They tingle from his touch and I can't help but trace my tongue where his lips were. He pulls me into him and I can feel his hard-on.

I squirm out of his embrace and take his hand. "Come on, let's go sailing.

His fingers entwine with mine and he rubs the pad of his thumb on my hand. It sends tingling sensations all through my body.

As he follows me up the wooden stairs, his hand shifts to my lower back. I feel him everywhere. I need to focus on something else. I don't need to be thinking about him touching me every chance he gets. I move out of his reach as he talks to the captain.

I make my way to the front of the boat, where there is a table set up with two glasses. There's a bottle of wine chilling. He's prepared his seduction well.

"Are you ready for a little fun?" he asks from behind me.

"This is really nice. Is it yours?"

"No, but I was thinking about buying it." He is watching me carefully. "Do you think I should?"

"I love it, but don't buy it because of me." He was given a huge monetary settlement from the Army, but the doctors explained it to him that it was an insurance settlement due to his wreck.

He doesn't say anything, he just points to the cushions to sit on. I sit and he pours us a drink as I feel the boat leave the dock. He must have prearranged this somehow with the Captain, to have an ice bucket to chill a bottle of wine for us.

"Thank you." I take the glass of wine he offers.He sits down close to me, but not touching me.

He leans back and stretches out his long muscular legs and my mouth waters.

"Sit back and relax. Enjoy the wind in your hair. It's a beautiful day."

I lean back next to him and close my eyes. I soak in the fact that, I'm sitting next to the man that I love. I'm terrified, yet at the same time, I feel a sense of happiness for the first time in a long time.

It couldn't last. We had to begin exploring the boat. We walk down to the cabin holding hands like lovers. As soon as we hit the landing in the cabin, he pulls me to him and kisses me.

I remember his tongue. How it used to slide with mine. How he used to taste.

His hand travels down my back to my ass. My fingers can't help but pull the curls at his neck, causing him to groan.

When our lips part, we are both breathless. My head clears enough for me to step away. "We can't do this."

"We won't do anything that you're not ready for, but please, understand that I feel like I've been waiting for you for a long time already."

"How can you feel that way when you've just met me?"

He pushes me gently toward the bed so I can sit down. He sits beside me, facing me. "I feel like I've known you for years. I can't explain it, but I feel pieces of you here." He takes my hand

and covers his heart with it. I choke back my emotions or I'd thrust myself into his arms.

"When I laid eyes on you in the restaurant that night, I felt like I knew you. I don't know how, but my heart and body belonged to you at that moment. I lied to you when I told you I wasn't on a date. But the minute I saw you, the date ended. I took her home and told her that my heart was already taken. She slapped me. I can't say that I didn't deserve it." He rubs his jaw as he remembers.

It scares the hell out of me that he knows these things about us. He isn't supposed to remember anything. He remembers feelings, he hasn't said that he actually remembers us being together. "I probably would have slapped you, too," I smile at him.

"No. I'm thinking that as feisty as you are, you probably would've kneed me in the balls." He laughs.

"You're probably right. But can we slow this down a bit? The last relationship I was in, moved so quickly. I fell so hard and fast." I can't look him in the face, I'm afraid he will see right through me.

He lifts my chin and our eyes lock. "I'm not that man. I don't want you thinking about anyone else when we're together." His eyes search mine for a response.

God, if he only knew what he was saying. I want the man he used to be, and I want the man he is now just as much. Together they are perfect.

"For now, can we go slowly and keep this between us? I don't want to be bombarded with questions from my family. We need time together before I can commit to anything."

"I'll give you whatever you need, baby." He softly kisses my forehead.

We spend the rest of the day sunning and enjoying each other's company. It's starting to get dark as we head back home. Kell is telling me how much he enjoyed our date as I catch headlights fall in behind us. As we make a turn, so does the car following us.

"Did you see that?" I ask him.

"I did. I'm going to slow down and see if the car passes us." He slows to half the speed and the car goes around us. Whoever it is, ducks his head as he passes us. He has a ball cap on blocking any facial features.

"There is no tag on the car. " I point out to him.

Kell doesn't increase in speed but the car ahead of us races off. "Aren't you going to chase him?"

"No, maybe it was a coincidence."

"This isn't a very high traffic area and he had no tag?"

"Why would someone be following us?" he looks my direction.

"I don't know, maybe it has to do with some job you're working?"

"Whoever it was is gone. There were no plates for me to run."

"I'm sure you're right." My gut tells me he's not.

As the fortress gate closes behind us, I watch in the mirror to make sure no one followed us. Once inside, I feel safe. I know Steel's security is solid. After we get out of the Hummer, we head to the steps of my home.

"Are you going to invite me inside?" he pulls me to him.

"I don't think that's such a good idea," I say as sweetly as possible to take the sting out of it for him.

"Can I see you tomorrow?"

"How about you come back out here? Bring your swimsuit and I will make you lunch."

"If you invite me inside, I won't have to come back in the morning," he says in that sexy tone of his.

"As good as that sounds that would not be going slowly." I smile up at him.

"Are you sure you are going to be okay out here all by yourself?"

"I will be fine. Steel has all kinds of security set up."

"Okay. I will make a sweep down the road, just in case we really were followed. Do you have a gun?"

I want to laugh.

If he could only remember how many guns I really do have or my sniper abilities, then he wouldn't have to ask.

"Yes, I am very well protected," I kiss his chin, "thanks for asking."

"Are you sure you're not up for a little make out session?" he presses into me.

"Goodnight, Kell."

"Goodnight, baby." He reluctantly releases me and climbs into his Hummer. I watch him as he leaves and make sure the security gate locks behind him.

CHAPTER

● crawl in bed wishing that Kell was with me. I try to convince myself that he will be okay. That the only memories he will have, will actually only be feelings. The feelings he has for me are strong. I love him so much and it took every ounce of strength in me to not let him come inside with me. If he touched me once more, I wouldn't have been able to tell him no.

"Are you asleep yet, baby?"

"Shit Kell, you have to stop scaring the hell out of me! Take me off your automatic frequency."

"I'm sorry. I will request you to answer from now on. Are you okay?"

"I'm fine. Did you see anything when you made your sweep?"

"Nothing other than whoever it was turned around and came back by. I followed the tire tracks until I got to the highway."

"I double checked all the security systems before I settled in."

"Chances of someone following you is slim. It's more than likely me, due to my line of work."

"I'm okay. Why are you linking with me?"

"I wanted to thank you for the day and to tell you how much I enjoyed your company."

"I should be thanking YOU."

"If you would've let me stay I could have come up with several ways for you to thank me."

Even his voice in my head sounds sexy.

"I'm sure that's very true," I remember all the things he used to come up with that brought us both pure pleasure. I'm unaware that I let out a soft groan.

"Baby, you make that sound again and I'm coming back over."

"Please…" I want him to, I want to lose control with him.

"Please what, baby?" he asks softly.

"Please don't." So not what I wanted to say.

"I get the feeling that you wanted to beg for something else," he says huskily.

"Good night, Kell, and don't forget to change your automatic controls on your link."

He growls and disconnects.

I wake with my body physically aching in all the places I dreamt that Kell touched me. It's going to be very difficult to keep him at arm's length for a month and I wanted to ravage him on the sailboat yesterday and stupid me invites him for a swim today. How will I ever avoid touching him shirtless? I stretch the ache from my body and hear Cy whining at the foot of the bed.

"I'm getting up. Not quickly, but I'm getting there."

He comes to the side of the bed and nuzzles into my touch. "What do you think? Am I being naïve in thinking everything will be okay?" He barks. "I know you worry about me. But I can't help myself, I love him." This time, he licks me.

"Okay…Okay… I'm getting up."

I crawl out of bed and make a pot of coffee. After letting Cy out, I hit the shower and put on my bathing suit and cover up. Rummaging around in the fridge, I find all the ingredients I need to make a chicken salad and a fruit plate. I hear my link beep and before I answer it, I know who it is and it makes me smile.

"Good morning, Kell! You're up early."

"I'm already on my way, I couldn't wait to see you."

I laugh. "Did you even sleep?"

"No. Every time I closed my eyes, a beautiful brunette made me hard."

"Who is she? I'll kick her ass." I tease him.

"Baby, there is no one but you I dream about. I even dreamt about you before I met you. Does that sound crazy? You were faceless, but I knew I'd know you on sight anywhere."

God, he is going to make this day so hard. "How far away are you?"

"I'll be there in five."

I watch on the monitor for him to arrive and remotely open the gate. Why am I so nervous? I feel like a school girl waiting for her first kiss. I open the door before he knocks. He walks right into my arms and kisses me sweetly.

"I missed you." He growls against my mouth.

He makes me breathless, but I manage to break free of his kiss. "Have you had coffee?"

"I would love to have coffee with you." He smacks a wet kiss on my lips.

"Are you always this happy in the morning?" I take his hand and lead him to the coffee mugs.

"You make me happy. " He grins.

Without asking, I put in a scoop of sugar and cream and hand it to him.

"How did you know how I drink my coffee?" he squints his brown eyes at me.

Shit! "I...um...guessed? I'm sorry I can fix you another cup." I try to hide my mistake.

"No, it's perfect. Really good guess, though."

"I've packed a picnic lunch for us to take down to the beach. Let me grab the cooler and a blanket."

"Let me help you."

I hand him the cooler and I load it while he stares at me.

"Is there something wrong?"

"Why do I get the feeling that you knew me before we even met?" he's frowning.

How the hell do I answer that? I take the cooler from his hand and set it on the ground. "I think deep inside, we always know the person that we will love before we even meet. Kismet. Karma. Serendipity. Whatever you want to call it."

His frown is replaced by his damn gorgeous smile. "So, you are saying that you love me?" He grabs me to him.

"I...I...think I love you?" Gah, I just keep getting in deeper.

"You think? After today, I want you to KNOW, because I intend to sweep you off your feet." He bends down and throws me over his shoulder and grabs the cooler and blanket with his free hand.

I'm giggling, "I didn't realize you meant literally sweep me off my feet." Cy starts dancing around us in circles while barking happily.

"It's okay, Cy. I promise not to drop her." He walks us to the cliff and puts me on my feet. He takes my hand and walks me down the rocky path. My dog has already beat us to the water and is swimming with Artemis, the seal.

I release his hand and feel the loss of his warmth. I spread the blanket out and take the cooler from him and place it next to the blanket. I watch as he peels off his shirt. Oh. My. God. He is so cut!

Syn said he'd been going to the gym.He is bigger than I remember him and he's still beautiful, despite some of the scars on his body. He stands there staring at me again.

"What?"

"Your turn, baby." He is gawking at me.

I keep myself fit, but next to him, I feel self-conscious. I slowly slip off my sandals and draw my cover-up over my head. I hear him inhale.

"God, you are even more beautiful than my dreams."

My face feels flush as his eyes travel over every inch of my body. "I'll race you to the water!" I don't give him time to respond, I take off for the ocean. He lets me win and dives underneath me. He comes up right in front of me, water dripping off his beautiful curls in his hair.

"I still won," he sputters.

"What? No, I beat you." I push his chest.

"I won because I got to watch that fine ass of yours while you were running."

"You have a one track mind don't you?" I feign displeasure.

"When it comes to you, yes I do. I call dibs on your entire body."

Artemis and Cy swim between us.

"You have a pet seal?" he laughs.

"He and Steel bonded when he moved here. She is somehow part of our crazy family. Don't ask. She actually thinks she's a dog, too. She plays fetch with them."

"I want to be part of your crazy family."

"Slow down. You and I talked about that, remember? For now, Syn doesn't need to know anything about us. Besides, I think I'm going to like sneaking around with you." I can't tell him that it reminds me of old times. "How about we enjoy today?"

We swim and play in the water, along with my dog and the seal, until we're both exhausted and finally collapse on the blanket. We lay beside each other holding hands. His thumb skims across my knuckles.

"Are you ready for some lunch?" I roll to my side to look at his beautiful sun-kissed face.

"I'm famished." He smiles.

I sit up and dig in the cooler to fix our plates. He rolls my direction so that he can look at me. I can see him watching me out of the corner of my eye. He licks his lips and it sends goosebumps down my body. "Could you stop that?"

"Stop what?" he laughs.

"Licking your lips. It's very distracting."

"You look...I mean lunch looks delicious." He continues to laugh at me.

"You look delicious, too. Yet I'm not over here drooling over you." I laugh at him.

"Why aren't you? I would gladly let you eat me up or better yet, I would gladly eat you up."

Gah! "Would you just sit there and behave?" I wave the butter knife at him.

"Okay. If you change your mind, I'm right here...all of me." He looks down to the bulge in his swim trunks.

He sees me admire him and I turn red. If he only knew how much I wanted to get my hands on him. "Here's your lunch." I shove his plate at him, with mock annoyance.

We eat our lunch together having great conversation. I love to watch him talk. Hell... I love everything about him.

"Have you ever been hang gliding?" he asks breaking my concentration on his lips.

"No. Have you?"

"It's settled then."

"Wait! What's settled?"

"Next weekend, I'm taking you hang gliding."

I can't help but smile at his enthusiasm. "That sounds like a lot of fun." I lay back down and he slides up next to me. His finger traces my belly button. It tickles and I giggle.

"That's a beautiful sound on you." He leans in and softly kisses my lips. "Have you fallen for me yet?"

I reach up and place my hand on his face and look into his eyes. "I already know that I love you. I just need some time for everything that comes with that."

"You mean sex."

"Yes," I exhale. "I can't explain it to you, but I don't think we are ready for that yet."

He leans his hard-on into me. "I think somebody is ready."

"Well, somebody is going to have to learn some control." I playfully scold him, followed by a laugh.

"I'll wait as long as you want, but I can't promise control when I finally get my hands on this gorgeous body of yours." He kisses my chin. "I'll be ready when you are."

Every part of me wants him right here and now. My control is wearing thin, but I need to give us more time. My hand itches to reach out and stroke him. Instead, I just say, "Thank you."

We pack up our things and head back to my house.

"Do you mind if I get in your shower?" He's stripping off his shorts as he walks.

I swallow hard and point him in the direction of the bathroom. He smiles and winks at me and heads into the shower. He doesn't shut the door behind him. My mind tells me to find something else to do, but my feet have already started moving toward the sound of the water. I stand in the doorway and stare at him. The steam has already started to cover the shower door. I watch the outline of him as he washes his body. Every inch of his body.

Without looking at me he says, "I know that you're watching me. You're more than welcome to join me."

I bite my lip to the point of pain and stop my hand just before I reach the shower door. I can't. I want to, but not yet. I turn and leave with a low aching in my belly. I work on cleaning up our picnic items. I have to get him out of here before my family gets back and sees him.

Kell comes back out with a towel wrapped around his waist. "I need my clothes." He points to his bag he left by the door. I'm frozen in place watching him lean down and pick it up. He knows what the hell he is doing to me because he is grinning from ear to ear as he walks back to the bathroom.

As I finish cleaning up, he comes back out fully clothed and damn it if it doesn't look just as gorgeous. I really have to get him out of here.

"I need to shower and change and head to work for a few hours."

He walks up to me and places his hands on my hips. "Is that your way of telling me that I need to leave?"

"I'm sorry. My family will be back soon. I don't want Syn to see you here."

He kisses my forehead. "I will keep our little secret for now, but eventually he needs to know because I plan on spending every free moment with you." He takes my hand and walks to the front door. My dog is at our feet.

"You take good care of her." He pats Cy on the head. "Don't forget we have a hang gliding date next weekend." He kisses me lightly on the lips.

"I won't forget. Thank you for this weekend."

"It was my pleasure. Well...I would have liked to make it more pleasurable for you, but I agreed to wait."

I laugh and direct him out the door and watch him drive away.

About an hour later, Steel, Ady, and Syn make it home. Syn stays just long enough to say hi to me and pet Cy, then leaves for home right away. Steel and Ady settle in to tell me all about their weekend. They caught a ton of fish and had a great time.

"You should come with us next time," Ady suggests. "We felt bad, you being left alone, while we had fun. Next time, you're coming along. No more sitting around moping.

"I will, I promise. You look exhausted."

"I didn't sleep much with two grown men sharing war stories all night."

"Get some sleep, we'll catch up tomorrow."

Pieces of Gray

CHAPTER

C y wakes me up barking. It's eight A.M. Someone is knocking on my door. I grab my robe and the knocking has turned to pounding. I hear Steel yelling for me to open the door.

I fling it open and Steel barges inside. "What is it? Did something happen to Ady?" He has me terrified.

"Sit down," he barks, "we need to talk."

"What is it, Steel? You're scaring me to death."

"I saw him here. I was checking my monitor because there was one warning lit up over the weekend. What the hell are you doing? Why was Kell here?"

I sit down on the couch and motion for him to join me. He is still furious, but he sits.

"He contacted me. He showed up at my work."

"Does Syn know?"

"No, I am not going to tell him. Look, I know the risks, I've done the research. I didn't seek him out, I was trying to get over him. He found me. He feels like he knows me, but he doesn't remember anything."

"Not yet, but when he does, it will be disastrous for both of you."

"I love him. God knows I've tried to stay away from him, but we are like magnets, drawn together."

Steel's face softens and he scoots closer to me. "I don't want to see either one of you hurt, but I don't think this is a good plan. I think Syn should know about it, too. Just so he will be able to watch for signs of his memory returning."

"I AM watching him! I'm being careful with him and going slow. He seems nothing but happy. Please, don't tell Syn!" I plead with him. "He'll just send him away."

He stands up. "Syn needs to know."

"What if it were Ady? Would you be willing to let her go if there were the slightest chance that you could have her back?"

He stares at me for the longest moment before he responds. "No."

I stand up in front of him. "Please just give us one last chance! Maybe he won't remember."

"I will keep your secret for now, but you have to promise me that if he starts to remember, then we will tell Syn."

I wrap my arms around his waist and hug him. "Thank you. I promise I will keep you posted."

He kisses the top of my head. "I don't like it one bit, but I understand loving someone so much that you would be willing to do anything to keep them. I would die before I would give up Ady again."

"You do understand, then. Syn doesn't know what it is like to love someone that much."

"If my brother keeps up his charming ways, then he may never know." He laughs.

I pull back from him. "Did you see anything else on the monitor? I looked when I felt like someone was watching me, but I didn't see anything. And then yesterday someone was following behind us in a car with no plates. Kell checked it out but wasn't able to trace anything. He felt like that in all likelihood, it might be someone following him because of his line of work."

"I didn't see anything on the monitor. But I will go back and check the street cameras to see if I can get a good look at the car and maybe the person driving it. In the meantime, you be careful and watch your surroundings, especially when you are around Kell."

"I will, and thanks again for not telling Syn about Kell."

Steel did see the car on the monitor twice, but the driver's face was turned away both times. He had extra cameras installed outside the perimeter further down the road, just to remove any blind spots. It made me feel better when he told me.

Kell checked in with me midweek. He let me know that he'd be tied up all week with casework. He wanted to assure me that he'd still see me on Saturday, no matter what. We set up where to meet so that he wouldn't come to my place again.

"Hey Adam," I greet him as he enters the door.

I had an early appointment with a woman wanting a dog for her son that just came back from war. I'd just finished with her.

"Hey, yourself." He smiles warmly at me. "Before I forget, there was some man here on Monday asking about you."

"Did he leave his name?"

"No. He was kind of odd. At first, he asked about the dogs and then he mentioned you by name. I gave him some basic info and then he asked about your family."

My heart starts racing. "Did you tell him anything?"

"No, I won't ever give out any personal information."

"What did he look like?"

"He was maybe in his early thirties, maybe 5'10" sandy colored hair. He kept his sunglasses on, so I couldn't tell you his eye color. Is there something going on that I should be aware of?"

"No. Just weird, I guess. I'm sure it was nothing." I walk in the back and sync up with Kell. I don't tell him about the man, but I ask about the car that followed us. He hasn't been able to track anything new down. I don't know why I didn't tell him, other than I don't want him to worry about me.

My day passes by uneventfully, except for the excitement generating through me about spending time with Kell tomorrow.

"How about having that dinner with me tonight?" Adam asks as he starts to lock up for the day.

I have to stop whatever he thinks I have started with him. "Can we go as just friends? Not a date? I like you, but I don't want this to end up being awkward between us, so I think it's safer for us just as friends."

He looks a little disappointed. "If that is all that you want, then yes."

We head out to the little café across the street. We order our food and he is very quiet.

"Do you want to ask me anything?" I hesitantly ask him.

"Why just friends?" He sips his water.

"There is someone that I have loved for many years. He has recently come back into my life."

"The guy that came in to see you last week?"

"Yes."

"Are you still in love with him?"

I want to be totally honest with him. "Yes."

"Okay. Thank you for telling me. I can't say that I'm not disappointed, but he's one lucky man." He smiles and tips his glass toward me.

"I'm so sorry. Until that night, I had no idea that I would ever see him again."

"Honestly, it's okay. Probably better off if we stay friends with our working relationship, anyway. But if he hurts you, then he'll have to answer to me." He winks at me.

"Thank you for being so understanding." Adam really is a nice guy. But, I think that even if Kell hadn't come back into the picture, it wouldn't change the fact that I only want to be friends with him.

117

We finish our dinner and I grab my dog and head home. As I drive, I'm very cautious to watch for lights to fall in behind me. I have no idea who was asking about me or why, but it has definitely made me a little paranoid.

The lights are still on at Steel and Ady's house. I think Steel should know about the man asking questions.

"Knock, knock…are you guys up?"

"Hey, Gray. We're in the kitchen." I hear Ady yell.

I walk in and it smells heavenly. "What smells so good?"

"Ady has been craving pumpkin bread." Steel laughs.

"Really, it's not even Fall for another month." I join Steel at the bar.

"This baby already has a mind of its own." She laughs. "You're welcome to help me eat it. It should be ready in about ten minutes."

"I would love to. In the meantime, can I steal your husband for a few minutes?"

"You okay?" she asks.

"Yeah, I just need to update him on some information."

Steel walks over and kisses her quickly. "We'll just be a minute. It's fine, nothing for you to worry about."

We walk outside out of Ady's ear shot. "What's up?" he looks concerned.

"Some man came by the training center on Monday. He was asking my boss questions about me and my family. Adam didn't tell him anything, but he said the man was acting weird. He never took his sunglasses off, so he doesn't have a good description of his face."

"So, now you're thinking someone is following you rather than Kell?"

"It would seem that way, but I don't know why someone would be following me"

"Are there any camera's at the training center?"

"Only inside the training areas."

"I think we need to involve Syn. This is his line of work."

"If we involve him, then he is going to find out about me seeing Kell."

"Sweetie, I don't think that is a bad thing." He rubs my arm.

"You know Syn will go crazy and move him. Please, don't tell him!" I'm begging him.

"Okay, we'll leave Kell out of it, but Syn can still do some investigating. You're still keeping a gun with you at all times, right?"

I pull my pistol from the back of my jeans. "Always."

"Good girl. You keep me updated if anything peculiar happens or I will tell Syn everything. I can't risk your safety for your secret."

"I will, I promise."

I spend the rest of the night watching Ady eat a whole loaf of pumpkin bread while we watch television. I want to tell her about Kell so badly, but for now, I need to keep it to myself. I love her like a sister. I hate hiding things from her.

I get the hint that it is time for me to leave when Steel cuddles up with Ady on the couch. The love between them is so sweet. I like seeing him happy and in love. This is what I want with Kell.

I wake up early with my dog curled into my side. I don't remember him crawling into bed with me. I jump up and hit the shower. I can't wait to see Kell today. As I'm getting out of the shower, my link connects.

"*Hey, baby. Have you left yet?*"

"I just got out of the shower. I'll be leaving in ten minutes."

"*That means you're naked.*" I hear him inhale deeply.

"No. No, I'm dressing as we speak."

"*I'm okay with naked hang gliding.*"

I can't help but laugh at him. "I'm sure you would be, but that's not happening."

"You've already given me a hard-on talking about being naked."

"You started it." I don't dare tell him that I'm soaked.

"Just get your fine ass here as soon as you can. I miss you."

"I've missed you, too. I'll be there shortly."

The drive to the cliffs is beautiful. Kell is leaning against his truck waiting for me. I put my Jeep in park and admire him for a minute. He is absolutely gorgeous. I love everything about this man. He slowly walks over and opens my door.

"Are you going to stare at me all day or are you getting out?"

I slide out of the Jeep. "I rather like staring at you."

"Baby, that look you are giving me says you want to devour me. If you don't stop, we are climbing back into your Jeep and I will gladly let you devour every part of me."

I feel a throbbing between my legs. I swallow hard, to focus. "As good as that sounds, I'm really looking forward to hang gliding with you."

His lips collide with mine as he kisses me deeply. "At some point, you will devour me and I will devour you." I feel his hand slowly run down my backside and squeezes when he gets to my ass.

"I…um…know you're right, but not today." That had to be the most painful thing I have ever said because there is nothing more I want than to feel him inside me again.

"Are you ready for our adventure?" He releases me, and I miss his touch.

"Yes."

We listen to the instructors and make our way over to the edge. We each have our own gliders. "You go first. " I tell him.

He takes off and I watch as he dips down and then glides back up over the horizon. "Oh my God! This is amazing!" I hear in my ear. "Come on, baby. You're going to love it."

I step up and jump off. It is the most incredible feeling. This is what it must feel like to fly. I catch up with him and we fly side by side. We point out mountains and waterways to each other. I love the feeling of floating and that I am experiencing this with him. We fly for almost an hour. He points out an area where he wants to land. It's a pebble beach cove surrounded by mountains.

We make our way down and I see a tree house tucked into the side of the mountain with a rickety bridge leading into the trees. "This place is beautiful."

"It's all ours for the night. I drove over last night and set up everything."

"I didn't realize we were staying the night. I didn't bring any clothes."

"You don't need clothes, but I did buy you some." He grabs me to him.

"What about my dog?"

"Call Steel and make up some story about why you can't make it home and he can take care of Cy for you."

"Steel knows about us."

"I thought you didn't want your family to know?" He frowns.

"He saw you on the monitor when you stayed the weekend. He has agreed to not tell Syn for now."

"Perfect, then you don't have to lie to him. Tell him you will be spending the night with the man you are madly in love with. That he will be doing all kinds of naughty things with you."

I smack him in the chest. "I thought we were going to take it slow?"

"We won't do anything you are not ready for, baby." He kisses me sweetly. "God, I hope you're ready for me."

We spend the rest of the day sunning and swimming. I am wearing the skimpy blue bikini he bought me. He had all our meals prepared and ready to go. The sun is starting to set and Kell turns on the twinkling lights that line the rickety bridge.

"I've never stayed in a tree house before," I say as I join hands with him.

"Me either. We have had lots of firsts today." He unclasps our hands and holds me to him. "I love you, Gray. I can't explain it, but I feel like I have loved you for years."

"I love you, too." I KNOW that I have loved him for years. "The sunset is beautiful here. How did you find this place?"

"A client of mine owns it. He never gets up here anymore, so he said I could use it anytime I would like."

"I would be okay if we hid out here forever," I sigh out.

"That sounds like a plan to me." His lips meet mine for a passionate kiss.

I tangle my fingers through his hair and he starts walking me backward into the tree house. I feel my legs hit the back of the bed. I don't want to resist him anymore. I break free of our kiss and raise my arms above my head. He doesn't hesitate at the invitation. His hands find the hem of my cover-up. He traces the edges with his fingers as his eyes scorch my skin.

"Are you sure, baby?" he whispers.

"Yes," I groan out as his hands run up my body stripping me.

After he removes my cover-up, he unties the strings that are barely holding up my swimsuit.

"You're beautiful and sexy as hell." He lifts me and places me on the bed as our tongues mingle. He steps back and removes his swimsuit and his erection is standing on his belly. "I need a condom." He starts to move away.

"I don't want anything between us. I promise I'm clean and I won't get pregnant." As I say the words, a sadness pulls at me.

He senses it. "What's the sadness I just saw flash in your beautiful eyes?" He lays down beside me and places his hand on my belly.

"Nothing. Please, just make love to me." I kiss him furiously.

"Baby, you never have to ask." He growls and his body covers mine.

My hands are all over him. I remember every inch of his body minus the scars. I push at his chest for him to roll over.I climb on top of him and start kissing each scar. My eyes start to water thinking about how he got them. He doesn't remember, but I do.

He sits up and we are face to face. "What is it, baby? Why the tears?" He places his hands on either side of my face. I can't escape him.

"It has been so long since I have made love to..." He covers my mouth with his swallowing my words. Thank God, because I almost finished that sentence with "you."

"I don't want to know who else you have made love to you. You belong to me now. You will never need or want any other man."

He was right the first time when he said those same words to me. I know he's still right. He kisses down my neck. My breasts are in his hands. I want to feel him inside me so badly.

I try to raise up, to put him inside me, but he rolls me off of him and has my legs spread wide. His tongue is as magical as ever. He licks and sucks until I scream his name.

Before I have fully come down from my orgasm, he rolls me over and has my ass in the air. He sinks inside of me and then pulls me up on my knees. I reach behind me and find his hair again and I pull it.

He growls and steadies my hips and pushes deeper inside me. He stills and his hands find my nipples. He pulls and rolls them and I can feel myself building again. He feels it too and pushes my belly back on the bed. His hand finds my sweet bundle of nerves. He rubs, then pumps into me. He repeats this several times and it's driving me crazy. He likes bringing me to the edge and stopping. It feels amazing.

I swear he has grown bigger inside me. I feel so full.

"Please!" I beg.

He flattens his hand in the middle of my back, as his other hand rubs me. "Come for me, baby."

My body does as it's told, and I come harder than I ever have before. I feel him pull out of me, and I wince. He sits back on the bed and pulls me onto his still hard shaft. I raise up and slowly lower onto him. His eyes stare into mine. His breathing has increased. He is fighting for control. I place my hands on his broad shoulders and I slowly ride him. I see him bite his lip. I release his lip with my teeth and I feel him start to shiver. I pick up my pace before he grabs my hips. Somehow, I am on my back and he is relentlessly pumping into me. It brings me to another orgasm and this time, his release follows with an animalistic roar.

We are both drenched, trying to calm our breathing. He rolls back and I lay my head on his chest. His hand rubs down my arm.

"That was fucking amazing," he says between breaths.

"It was. You can do that to me anytime."

He rolls me off of him and faces me. "How come I feel like your body is home to me? I know you, I know your noises, and I know what pleases you. I know that when my fingers trace your belly button, it drives you crazy. How is this possible?"

I want to tell him that it was always that way between us. He knew my body the first time he touched me. "I…I don't know, but I'm very happy that you do." I try to tease him a little to cut through the seriousness etched on his face.

He smiles, "I'm glad you knew my body, too." He kisses me and slowly makes love to me again.

Morning comes too early, but I can't remember the last time I slept so peacefully. I feel for Kell next to me. His side is empty. I sit up and I see him standing outside on the rickety bridge. I watch him for a moment. He is staring out into the distance. It unsettles me. I grab his shirt off the floor and slip it over me.

"Kell." He doesn't' respond. I slip my arms around his waist and he jumps. "I'm sorry, I called your name. Are you okay?"

"Yeah, I'm sorry, I woke up with a bit of a headache. My mind feels a little foggy." He turns in my arms and holds me.

I'm scared shitless. "What do you mean by foggy?" I don't look up at him.

"It's hard to explain. It's like I'm supposed to remember something, but I can't bring it into focus."

Shit, shit, shit! I knew it was too soon. "How about some coffee and Tylenol?" I turn away from him so that he can't see the fear on my face.

"I'll take you up on the Tylenol, but I think I'm going to lay down for a little bit. I didn't sleep well. I'm sure that's all it is. The hang gliding team isn't scheduled to pick us up for another couple hours.

He takes the Tylenol and lays down. He's asleep within a few minutes. I sit on the side of the bed and watch the soft rise and fall of his chest. He has a crease in his brow. I just want to be next to him. I am so empty without him, I don't want to let him go again. I want to lay by his side, to be next to him, to make sure he's alright. I want to take care of him. I lay next to him making sure to not touch him. The feelings I have for him are so overwhelming. God, I hope I didn't push him too far or too soon.

I lay still for the next hour and watch him sleep. The crease in his brow is gone. I move to quietly get off the bed before I feel his hand barely touch mine.

"Where are you going?"

"I didn't mean to wake you. Are you feeling better?"

He rubs his hands over his face. "Yeah, my headache is gone. Crawl back in here with me. I want to feel your heartbeat next to mine."

Oh my God! I love this man. I refuse to lose him again. I peel off his shirt and lay skin to skin with him and my heart beats in rhythm with his. This is such a sweet moment with him that I don't ever want to forget it.

CHAPTER 13

"Steel? I've just made it home. Can I come talk to you?" I ask through my link.

"Yeah, we were getting ready for bed. Come on over," he answers.

"It can wait until tomorrow."

"Gray, get your ass over here!" he barks and disconnects.

"Come on, Cy. You can play with Archeron and Styxx, while I chat with Steel." He follows in right behind me. We make it to the front door as Steel opens it.

"I was headed over to you because I figured you weren't coming," he says as we pass through the door.

"Where is Ady?" I whisper.

"She's brushing her teeth. Come here and sit down and tell me what's going on?"

"I think I made a huge mistake," I whisper as I sit down beside him.

"Tell me what happened." His voice is laced with concern.

"I spent the weekend with Kell...

In a treehouse...

Alone the entire weekend..."

"You spent last weekend with him here alone, so what's the difference?"

"We...we had sex," I say the last part a little too loud.

"Who did you have sex with? And why are telling Steel instead of me?" Ady giggles as she enters the room.

Steel and I both look at each other not knowing what to say.

"What are you two up to?" Ady laughs as she plops down on the couch beside us. We both remain silent. "Come on you two, spill it." She points her finger between the two of us. "Oh, was it the guy you work with?" She is all smiles.

"You should tell her. She's not going to give up until she knows." Steel stares at me.

"It was...Kell." I say it and hold my breath for the wrath of both of them to come down on me.

"Kell. As in Kell Crew, who you're never supposed to see again?"

"One and the same," I answer.

She narrows her eyes at Steel. "And you knew about this?"

"Ady, this is all my fault," I insist. "Kell spent the weekend here last week while you guys were on your fishing trip. When Steel checked the monitor he saw Kell here."

She gets up off the couch. "Does Syn know? Because I'm pretty sure if he did, you would never see Kell again." She's pacing, but speaking quietly.

Steel stands to join her. "We decided to keep it a secret for now and wait and see how Kell progresses." He stops pacing and looks back at me. "Wait, did something happen after you had sex with him?"

"That's what I came over here to tell you. He woke up this morning with a headache and said that things seemed a little fuzzy. I gave him some Tylenol and he took a nap. When he woke up, he was fine." My voice quivers, "I'm so scared I'm going to lose him again."

Ady sits back down beside me. "Sweetie, maybe it was nothing." She hugs me and my tears start to fall.

Kelly Moore

"I know that I was willing to risk my life to be with him—but now I think I just risked his." I'm in full panic mode now.

Steel comes and kneels in front of me. "Gray...we need to tell Syn."

The tears fall harder. "I know."

"Why can't it wait a little longer," Ady chimes in. "Maybe his headache was just a headache and nothing more."

I sniff unladylike. "Do you think so?"

"No," Steel answers. "You two do not make light of this. This could be the beginning of him remembering."

"And, it could be a simple headache." Ady meets Steel on her feet.

I stand up. "I don't think Syn would understand. He has never been in love with anyone."

"Syn has put his life on the line for both of us. It doesn't matter that he hasn't been in love before, he knows how to love and he loves deeply."

"I know you're right, but I don't think I can survive losing him again. I've tried for years to get over him and move on with my life. I don't think there is any other man for me." I sob again.

"Just like there would be no other man for me if something happened to you, Steel," Ady adds.

I see his face soften a bit. "So, what are you two proposing that we do?"

Ady starts pacing again. "Lay low this week, don't see him only talk to him through your link. Ask him if he has had any more headaches? Touch base with Syn. He updates you on Kell. Ask him how Kell is doing." She stops pacing.

I hold my breath, my eyes pleading with Steel.

"One week, that's it. If he shows any more changes, I will tell Syn myself and you two ladies will have to be mad at me." He turns to point his finger at us.

"Deal," we both say in unison.

"Thank you. I love you both."

128

"Now tell me a little about this hot sex you were having," Ady says smiling.

I start laughing. Steel's face turns red. "Ignore her, it's the pregnancy hormones."

"I think I should leave, so you can tend to your wife's needs," I say laughing and heading for the front door. "Come on, Cy. I think they need some alone time, again."

My link buzzes as I climb into bed. *"Hey beautiful, I wanted to make sure you made it home safely."*

"I did. Thank you for this weekend. Any more headaches?" I ask.

"No."

"Do you get them very often?" I don't know what I'm hoping he will say.

"I use to get them more frequently. I never told you, but I was really sick. I kept putting off going to the doctors. When I finally did, I drove myself and I passed out in the car and wrecked. That's how I got my scars and my voice changed due to vocal cord damage from my infection. Right after all that happened, I'd get headaches every couple of days."

"Do you remember your accident?" I want to know how in-depth they went in adding memories.

"It's funny. I feel memories of you, but we have never met. I don't feel memories of the accident or being sick, but they both actually happened."

"Maybe that's your minds way of making you forget." What he feels for me is so much deeper than the memories they planted in his brain. That's interesting to know.

"You're probably right, it's just weird."

There is an awkward silence between us for a moment. *"I loved making love to you this weekend. I want to be in your bed every night, holding you."*

Gah, I want the same thing, too. "That can't happen right now. I still don't want Syn to find out about us. We have to be more careful. It will be more difficult over the next several weeks to see one another. I've picked up extra shifts at the hospital. It's our busy season and we're shorthanded." I had to make up some believable excuse.

"That's not what I wanted to hear." He breathes out.

"I know, I'm sorry. I will miss you if that makes you feel any better." That's the truth, I miss him every moment we're not together.

"I'll miss you, too. Did we move too quickly? Did I scare you away?" he asks sadly.

"We did move a little quicker than I had planned, but I don't regret one moment with you. I'm a little scared, but not of you. I'm scared of the feelings I have for you." This is as honest as I can be with him.

"Sometimes I'm afraid of how much I feel for you, too. But I'm not going to back away from it. I love you."

"I love you, too."

I dive into work this week. Kell and I have spoken on the phone every night and he honestly seems okay. I promised Steel and Ady that I would check in with Syn to see if he has noticed anything. I linked with him last night and set up a lunch date with him at a café around the corner from his office.

"Hey, sweetheart." He kisses my cheek.

"Thanks for making time to have lunch with me."

"I thought I might have to cancel we've been so busy this week."

"I'm glad your business is going so well. How is Kell?"

The waitress interrupts us to take our order.

"Are you sure you want to know?" His brow creases.

"Yes, I'm sure." I touch his hand.

"I think he is seeing someone," he says softly.

I choke on my water I was sipping. "What makes you think that?" I ask through coughs.

"I knew I shouldn't have said anything." He hands me a napkin.

"No, no it's fine. Please, tell me."

"He's happier than I've ever seen him." He hesitates. "He doesn't ask about you anymore." He looks sad as he says the words. "I don't say that to hurt you, but maybe it will make you finally move on. I think you have been holding onto the thought of getting him back."

God, I want to tell him so badly. I hate lying to him. "I'm glad he's doing well. You haven't seen any signs of him gaining any of his memories back?"

"Nothing that I have noticed or anything that he has complained about."

Our order comes and the rest of our conversation is light. I steer away from anything else concerning Kell. It turns my stomach to be lying to Syn. He's done everything he can to protect me and to help Kell. I feel like such an asshole.

"Syn...I..."

"What is it?"

I almost tell him, but choke back the words. "I don't want you to worry about me anymore when it comes to Kell. I'm fine." That is the only truth I've told him today.

"I'm glad to hear it, and I'm sorry I had to be the one to tell you that he's moved on."

If Kell had really moved on, this conversation would be devastating. I would definitely not be okay. "I'm glad to hear that he is happy." Another truth.

Out of the corner of my eye, I see a vaguely familiar face. I lean in so I can whisper to Syn. "The guy sitting up at the bar. I feel like I know him from somewhere."

He turns to look. "That's Private Daniel Davis's brother. We met him at the funeral."

"That's right, I think his name is Douglas. They were from Portland area weren't they?"

He recognizes us and comes up to our table. Syn and I both stand. "I remember you two," he says and shakes Syn's outstretched hand.

"How are you doing?" I ask him.

"I'm doing okay, thanks for asking. I'm in town doing some research."

"I want you to know that your brother was a brave man and again, I'm very sorry that we weren't able to get to him in time," Syn says.

"I hear that the soldier you did rescue is doing well." He looks between us.

"Yes, he has been able to put his life back together due to new technology for PTSD patients."

"I sure wish my brother would have had the same opportunity," he states flatly.

I see a slight change in his demeanor. I touch Syn's arm. "We are truly sorry for your loss. Syn, I really need to get going."

"Of course, thank you for your time. Please tell the other soldier that survived, that I'm sure my brother would wish him well." He turns and leaves the café.

"That was weird," I tell Syn.

"What do you mean?"

"Didn't you see him change when he was talking about his brother and Kell?"

"I saw a man that mourns the loss of his brother." Syn waves at the waitress for the check.

"I don't know, Syn. I have been trained to read people very well. It was part of my sniper training to read the slightest differences in people. Something about him just felt off."

"I didn't get the same vibe. I think you are being a little paranoid about it." He pays the bill and we head to our cars.

"I wonder what type of research he's doing?"

"Let it go, Gray. He just misses his brother." He leans in and kisses my forehead.

"I guess you're right. Thanks for lunch." My gut tells me differently, but I have enough on my plate to worry about with Kell.

CHAPTER

14

I've been able to stave off Kell for two weeks, but he's not having it anymore.

"I want to see you, tonight," he demands.

"Okay, how about you come to my place? I'll cook you dinner?"

"And dessert?" I can hear him smile.

"We'll see about dessert. Can you be here at seven?"

"I'll be there. Just so you know, I'm packing an overnight bag." he growls.

"I fully expected it." I laugh at him.

I make quick plans to invite Steel and Ady. Neither one of them has ever had the opportunity to really meet Kell. I want them to see what I see in him. I want them to love him as much as I do and then, maybe they could help me to break the news to Syn. I don't want to continue to lie to him.

"We would love to officially meet him." Ady sounds excited over the link.

I hear Steel mumble something in the background.

"My husband will also be on his very best behavior, unless he wants to sleep on the couch," I hear her threaten my cousin.

"Does he not want to meet him?"

"He does…he just wants you to be okay. He doesn't want Syn to kill us all when he finds out about it."

"I was hoping after the two of you get to know him, that you could help me tell Syn."

"Strength in numbers," she adds. *"That's a good plan."*

"Yeah, something like that." I laugh. "Tell Steel, I had lunch with Syn and he says that Kell is happier than he's ever been. No signs of distress."

"I'll tell him. What time do you want us there?"

"I told Kell seven, so maybe seven thirty. It will give me time to break it to him that we won't be alone."

She laughs. *"I'm sure that will be a disappointment. We'll be there."*

Fall has finally hit and I get to dig out my boots. I love tall boots in the fall and winter with leggings and a soft flowing dress. I get to leave my long hair down more this time of year.

Just as I finish brushing it out, I hear the gate monitor beep. He's right on time. I'm so excited about seeing him, I decide to meet him out front. He hops out of the Hummer and whistles at me.

"Woman, I love you in those kickass boots." He picks me up and spins me around. "Two weeks is too damn long." He kisses me deeply as he sets my feet back on the ground. "I've missed you."

"Hey, I've missed you, too." I twine my fingers with his and lead him inside.

Cy greets him inside the doorway. He pats him on the head. "Yes, I've missed you, too."

"Would you like a drink?" I ask as I head for the kitchen. He's right behind me and places his hands on my ass. He leans in and nips my ear and I feel a twinge of excitement between my legs.

"I was hoping for dessert first," he says in that sexy as hell gravelly voice.

"You're out of luck for now. Steel and Ady are joining us for dinner."

"I'd like to say that I'm disappointed, but I'm actually happy about spending time getting to know your family. Does that mean we get to tell Syn soon?"

"Let's see how tonight goes first." I turn and kiss him softly. "They'll be here in about thirty minutes."

He wraps his arms around me, trapping me against him. "You know—we could have a pretty sweet dessert in thirty minutes."

He doesn't make this very easy, either that or I'm just easy with him. "I promise dessert later, but I need to finish cooking. How about you put your feet up and enjoy the view."

I pour him a rum and coke and hand it to him. "I think I could handle the view from back here." He swats my ass.

"Behave, I'd hate for you to have a raging hard-on when Steel and Ady walk in."

"This is true. What are you cooking, wench?" He laughs and sits down.

"Homemade chicken pot pie. I need to brown the crust and it will be ready. Could you toss the dressing in the salad?" I bend over to put the pot pie under the broiler.

"You keep bending over like that and I'll do anything you want, Baby."

He looks sexy as hell standing at the bar mixing the salad. Just as I lose all my remaining willpower and I'm ready to give in to him, I hear Steel and Ady come through the front door. Damn it.

"We're in the kitchen!" I yell. Kell suddenly looks a little nervous. I don't think I've ever seen him nervous.

He puts out his hand to Steel and then Ady moves in to hug him. "It's so nice to meet you," she says.

Steel places his hand on Ady's shoulder. "You'll have to forgive her, the pregnancy makes her emotional."

Pieces of Gray

"I'm not emotional." She sniffs and she leans into Steel's embrace.

"How far along are you?" Kell points at her belly bump.

"Four more months to go," Steel answers proudly and rubs her belly.

"This is your first, right? Boy or girl?" Kell asks.

"Yes, this is our first. My sweet hubby is being old fashioned and doesn't want to know the sex of the baby," Ady answers. She leaves Steel's arms and heads around the bar. "Can I help with anything?"

"Why don't you two go relax on the couch, while we finish up in here," I say as I hand Ady dishes to set the table. It's such an open area, it's hard not to pay attention to what the boys are talking about.

"He's gorgeous," Ady whispers.

"Don't let Steel hear you say that, he'll throw him out on his ear," I laughingly warn her.

"Well, you never told me he was THAT good looking. So, forgive me for noticing. A girl would have to be blind not to notice him," she teases me. I laugh along with her.

I lean back on the counter and watch him for a moment. "It's not just that he is gorgeous. I've grown up around some nice looking men and worked and fought next to them and not been attracted to them. I'm drawn to him like no other man. His soul speaks to mine and has wrapped around my heart."

"I know that feeling very well." Ady sniffs again as she looks at Steel. She waves her hand in the air, "Steel is right, it's the hormones."

"What you feel for Steel isn't the hormones, and you know it. I'm glad you understand how I feel because then you can understand why I couldn't stay away from him. I'm afraid that Syn won't be as understanding."

"Syn wants the two of you to be happy and healthy. You know, the two of them have really become very good friends."

"I know. He's going to feel so betrayed by us. Just the thought breaks my heart."

"Let's not worry about Syn tonight. Let's get to know that hot sexy man of yours."

Steel and Kell hit it off right away. Our dinner conversation was full of laughter and it felt so comfortable. The boys actually made a date to go fly fishing together. Ady and Kell take Cy outside while Steel helps me with the dishes.

"I like him. You two are perfect for one another." His eyes look a little haunted.

I turn to face him. "But?"

"I know you love him, but I'm scared for you. This could all fall apart so quickly. I've seen you struggle over the last year trying to move on and now you feel like you have another chance with him. What happens to you if he remembers everything and can't handle it again?"

"I'm more worried about what happens to him if he remembers. He has no one. I have all of you."

He steps closer. "You do have all of us that love you, but that didn't help you get over him before."

"Even when I thought he was dead, I never got over him. I just learned to live without him, but he's not dead, and I don't want to be without him."

He hugs me to him. "We'll figure it out, but Syn needs to be brought up to speed. The sooner, the better."

"Will you go with me to tell him?" My eyes plead with his.

"If you need me to, then you know I will."I give him a tight hug.

Ady interrupts us. "What's all this hugging I'm missing out on in here?" She joins our embrace.

I can't help but laugh at her. "I think it's time you took your wife home and show her a little affection, Steel. She's getting needy."

She kisses his lips quickly. "I agree," she says beaming at him. He gives a lusty laugh of agreement and pulls her toward the door.

As they pass by Kell, Steel calls back to me, "We'll talk some more tomorrow." And then to Kell he says, "We'll firm up the date for our fishing trip later."

"Goodnight", they both say as the door shuts behind them.

"What was that all about?" Kell asks as he strolls toward me. "They left in a hurry."

"It's about love, and hormones. Right now, mainly her hormones." I laugh.

"I like hormones," he says as he reaches me. His eyes have dilated.

"I can see that." I glance down at his crotch.

"Tonight was great, but I've had a hard-on since I laid eyes on you." His eyes skim every inch of my body. "I want to divest you of everything covering your gorgeous body." He kisses the sensitive skin right under my ear.

"You waste no time," I hiss in pleasure.

"I want all the time that I can get with you. It has been two weeks you've kept me waiting. " He picks me up and wraps my legs around his hips. Planting his hands firmly on my ass, he walks me to the stairs. We only make it a few steps, before he moans between kisses and sets me on a step. He comes down on top of me. "I'm not going to make it up the stairs. I need to be inside you right now."

His lips and teeth find their way to my erect nipples, as his hands are removing my boots. I'm frantically trying to reach the hem of his shirt to pull it over his head. He growls again and leans up. He pulls off my boots and removes my tights. While he rips his shirt off, over his head, my greedy fingers have unbuckled his jeans and found my way inside. He is so damn hard.

He jerks my hands away and pins them over my head. "You missed the part where I said I needed to be inside you now!" He puts my hands together in one of his hands remaining over my head. His other hand reaches down between my throbbing legs. "Good, you're already wet." Without another word, he pushes hard into me. I gasp at the quick fullness and he stills. "Are you with me, baby?" he rasps out as his mouth meets my nipple again, pulling hard. It doesn't hurt, it makes my need for him stronger.

"Yes!" I yell.

He pulls out and then pushes back in hard. He repeats this several times. Then in one motion, he stands with me, not breaking our connection. I wrap my arms around his neck and enjoy riding him as he moves us up the stairs. He sits on the edge of the bed and lays back, before raising his arms above his head. I run my hands down his chest and raise up and touch where we are connected. He lets out a hissing noise that makes me lose control. I grab his hands like he did mine and bite his nipple. He hisses again and I come undone around him. My orgasm takes over and it's all I can do just to hang on. He takes advantage of the moment and flips us over and loses his own control. I feel a sheen of sweat over his body as he lays on top of me.

"I'm sorry that was so quick," he whispers as he kisses my neck. "I needed you so badly."

My heart is so full of love for this man it aches. "You have all night to make it up to me." I wiggle my hips underneath him.

"I plan on doing just that."

CHAPTER

'm startled awake when I hear my name screamed. Kell is sitting straight up in the middle of the bed. He is soaked in sweat and is shaking. His eyes are wide open with fear and he keeps yelling out my name.

I sit up beside him, but I don't touch him. "I'm right here, Kell." He looks around the room and for a minute, I think he hears me.

"I told you to not give away your position on the roof. Do you have any idea what they will do to you! You should have let him kill me!" Tears are streaming down his face.

Terror has overtaken me. I have no idea what to do. Do I wake him, or do I let him work his way through his dream? I want to hold him and let him know it's not real, but it was real. What the hell have I done?

He lays back on the bed and closes his eyes. I see him shiver. Then he seems to settle down and be peacefully asleep again. Cy starts whimpering at the foot of the bed. I carefully crawl out, trying not to wake him. I leave to take the dog out of the room.

He hops on the couch with me and lays his head in my lap. I still have a chill down my spine at his screams. He's remembering and I'm going to lose him again. How am I going to help him if I fall apart? I should have never let him in again. God, what am I going to do? I curl up with Cy beside me and cry myself back to sleep.

"Hey beautiful, what are you doing down here? Did I snore?"

I wake to the sound of his voice and his hand running down my arm. I shoot up off the couch. "Are you okay?"

"I'm fine." He's scowling with confusion. "Why do you ask?"

"Don't you remember?"

"Remember what?"

"You had a nightmare," I say softly.

"No, I don't remember anything." He rubs his face. "Is that why you're down here? You should have woken me up." He runs both his hands down my arms. "I'm sorry if I kept you up."

"No. No, you didn't. You...you're sure you don't remember anything?"

"Baby, the last thing I remember was you falling asleep, exhausted in my arms after your third...no fourth orgasm." He nips my ear.

Relief washes over me. Is it a sign that he is beginning to remember? I really could use Aunt Brogan to pick her brain. Maybe I will link with her on the computer later.

"Baby, are you okay? I swear you just shivered." He leans back to look at me.

"It was a long night. How about I make us some coffee?" I slip from his arms and head to the kitchen and he follows me.

"I can't stay today. We have been busy in the field this week. I need to catch up in the office."

"It's okay, I have some research of my own to do." He turns me in his arms and kisses me.

"How about a shower before you make that coffee?"

"A hot shower sounds good, but I'm exhausted from all your love making and lack of sleep last night. Not that I'm complaining."

"What if I promise to behave and just wash you?"

"Now THAT I could handle." He takes my hand and leads me back upstairs. He turns on the hot water as I get us some towels. We undress and climb in letting the heat soak in. He holds me briefly and then proceeds to wash my entire body. I don't want him to know how turned on I am. I close my eyes and enjoy the feel of his hands.

I hear him chuckle and I peek at him with one eye. "What's so funny?"

"You don't realize the noises you make when I touch you. I can tell you're as turned on as I am, but I promised to only bathe you."

Bastard. He does know me well. I watch as he takes his hand and strokes his cock. I like watching him. I hear the noises he makes as well. I can tell by his sounds that he doesn't enjoy it as much as when my hand is stroking him.

"Let me," I whisper. He removes his hand and I cover his cock with mine and I stroke him firmly, mimicking what he was doing. The pitch of his moan changes to a familiar sound. I continue to stroke him hard until his release.

"God, I love you. Not just because of the great sex we have, I love spending time with you and I love the person inside here." He touches my heart with the palm of his hand.

I hide my fear engulfing him in a kiss. "I love you, so much."

As soon as I send him on his way, I sit in front of the computer debating hitting the link button to Aunt Brogan. My fear finally wins out and I hit the connect button. Her face lights up my computer.

"Hey, Sweetie! How are you?"

"I'm okay, but I really need your help." A tear rolls down my cheek.

"What is it, Gray?" Her brows knit together on the computer screen.

I catch her up on Kell. I tell her about the headaches and the nightmare. In between sobs, I justify what I have done by telling her how much I love him. What amazes me about Aunt Brogan is that she doesn't judge me.

"I will do some research on his symptoms and speak with his specialist. Give me a few days to get back with you on it. And Gray—I would have done the same thing. I learned a long time ago that if two hearts are meant to be together, they will find a way even if time passes between them. That love you feel for them can't be replaced by another person and you two have that same kind of love. He found his way to you once. You did what you had to do for him and yet he found his way back to you again. I think if they erased his memories a hundred times, he would still find you. He would always carry pieces of you with him."

"Oh, Aunt Brogan! Thank you for not beating me up, I've done that to myself enough. Please, don't tell my mom and dad yet. I need to tell Syn first. I don't think he is going to be as easy on me as you have been."

"I don't imagine any of this has been easy for you. I know my son can be headstrong, but he loves you and his brother fiercely. I know he just wants to protect you."

"That's what I'm afraid of. He will think he knows what's best for me, and send Kell away. He has no idea what it feels like to need and want someone so badly that you would risk everything for them."

"He does know. It is a different kind of love, but he would give his life for any one of us. Give him time to figure it out. None of us really know what the right answer for Kell is. We thought erasing his memory would cure him, but it didn't cure him of you."

"Thank you. I will call mom and dad and fill them in soon. Let me know what you find out from his doctor. I love you."

"Love you, too."

Sometimes I forget the story of my aunt and uncle. I can't imagine them not together. I know they were apart for three years

144

before they found their way back to each other by fate, and they have been inseparable ever since. Maybe she's right. It wouldn't matter, Kell would always find me.

I walk over to Steel's house and update him on Kell's nightmare. We both agree that we will meet with Syn by the end of the week. I want to get answers from Aunt Brogan first. I spend the rest of my day curled up on the couch with Ady watching old movies.

Steel waits on us hand and foot making sure we are both relaxed and comfortable. He periodically walks by and rubs her belly and kisses her. My heart aches at the thought that I'll never have children, but I'm so happy for them and I can't wait to spoil the baby rotten.

"So, have you agreed on any names yet?" I ask as Steel finally sits down between us and rubs Ady's feet.

"If it's a boy, we have agreed to name him Kyren," he says.

"After your dad. He'd love that," I add.

"We haven't agreed on a girl's name yet," Ady says. "Steel likes Lauren and I like Esme."

"What is it with you and old fashioned names, songs, and movies?" I playfully punch Steel in the arm.

"I guess I'm just an old soul. I was born in the wrong era." He laughs and rubs his arm. I didn't punch him that hard, he's just playing.

"That is just one of the many things I find endearing about you, old man." Ady leans up and kisses him.

"Gah, you two can't keep your hands off each other for more than five minutes." I get up to leave. "Please, don't ever change." I wink at them and head back to my place.

I can't shut my mind off. Every time I close my eyes, I see Kell waking from his nightmare he had while he was here the other night. Just as I am finally dozing off, I see my computer link light up. I jump out of bed at Aunt Brogan's face.

"Hey, did you find out something already?"

"I did and I'm sorry it so late, but I figured you wouldn't mind."

"No, no not at all."

"I was able to reach Kell's doctor today. Of course, he was very disappointed to hear that you two have reconnected, but he says that the nightmares are normal, as long as they don't remember them when they wake up. The memories are tucked way down in the brain and they should only come up as he dreams," she explains.

"He said to tell you to not ever wake him up while he is having them, it could be catastrophic for him. His brain may not let him move beyond the dream. Essentially, he would be stuck in time, reliving that nightmare all over again. He also said that Kell has not kept any of his follow-up appointments and he should really be checked out, especially given the new circumstances."

"You mean because I'm back in his life," I say softly.

"Yes, you know how I feel about it. But medically, the doctor has a right to be concerned about him," she adds as gently as possible.

"I know you're right. I'll have to find a way to convince him to see his doctor. Thank you for letting me know so quickly."

"You're welcome, Sweetie. Take care of yourself and don't forget to tell your mom and dad. I don't like keeping secrets from them, especially when it comes to our children."

"I promise, I will as soon as I've told Syn."

I'm not looking forward to that. I'd rather face a firing squad. And I just might be.

146

CHAPTER

I t's midweek before Steel and I decide to meet for lunch to decide when and where to tell Syn about Kell. The restaurant is packed. Steel is already seated in the back tucked in a booth.

"Wow, the food here must be really good to be this busy for lunch," I say as I slip in across from him.

"They have the best chicken wings here that I've ever had."

"I've walked by here many times but never stopped. I can't believe I've missed out. I love chicken wings."

"I know that's why I chose it," he smiles and the waitress walks up to get our order.

By the time our order arrives, I have filled Steel in on what his mother found out and that Kell has been skipping out on his appointments.

"Oh my God! These are the best," I say with a mouthful of food."

"I told you," he says with a knowing smirk. "Oh, yeah! I forgot to tell you that before you walked in here, I met a friend of yours," he says licking the sauce from his fingers.

"Oh really, who?"

"I think he said his name was Douglas."

I stop mid chew. "Douglas Davis?"

"Yeah, that was his name." He continues to delve into his wings.

"What did he say?" My gut tells me to be cautious.

"He just said that he was friends with you and Syn and he was here doing some research."

I wipe my hands with my napkin and sit back. "I wouldn't really consider us friends. His twin brother is the other soldier that we found still alive when we rescued Kell. He died before we made it back."

"He didn't mention that. Why do you look so worried?"

"I don't know, it's a gut feeling. Syn and I ran into him too and at the mention of his brother and Kell, his body language changed. Syn said I was being paranoid."

"He's probably still mourning the loss of his brother. I know if I lost Syn, I'd never be the same."

"I understand that, but my gut still tells me there's something more."

"Do you want me to check into it? I can do a background check and see what he's been up to since the death of his brother."

"Yes, I would. Especially if it has anything to do with Kell. I've messed up enough, I don't need him conveniently 'bumping' into him and asking him questions."

I don't think it's any coincidence that so many people I'm close to have now met this Douglas, someone I barely know. And I also don't like how he tells them he's friends with me and Syn, when he's not. Only he's not stalking Syn, as far as I know, he's only stalking me. Does he know about me and Kell?

Steel's voice snaps me back.

"Consider it done. Now about Syn, I think we should invite him over for dinner to our house. I want to make it about family. I've already made arrangements for my mom and dad, and yours to be flown in Friday."

"I haven't even told my parents yet. I wish you would've talked to me first." I'm irritated.

"I think it would be better to tell them all at once for their support. My mom is very good at reigning in Syn. You know, your mom and dad may also be concerned, but they'll support you."

"I hope you're right. What about Kell being there?"

"I don't think that's a good idea."

"I want him to meet my family. How about I invite him over for dessert after we have told everyone?"

"I'll leave that up to you. Now, if you aren't going to eat those wings, hand them here." He reaches for my plate.

"Touch my plate, and I will stab you with my fork." I raise it at him.

"You'd stab me over some food?" he laughs.

"Absolutely." I laugh back at him.

"Did you guys have a good flight?" I ask as my mom and dad hug me.

"We did, but I'm glad my feet are back on the ground."

Mom has never enjoyed flying. "I'm so happy you're all here. I've missed you."

"We've missed you, too."

Uncle Kyren and dad grab our luggage and we all pile into my Jeep. They're all firing off a million questions at once. I can hardly keep up. Besides, I really don't want to tell them anything until we are all at Steel's house. Mom wants to know if I'm dating anyone, I skirt her question to answer dads about work.

As we finally make it to the gated entrance to home, Syn is pulling in at the same time we are. I walk in to see if I can help Steel and Ady while the others catch up. Ady is mixing something in a bowl, she turns when she hears me walk in.

"Are they all here?" she asks.

"Yeah, Syn met us out front, and they're all settling in and catching up."

"Are you nervous?"

"A little—but I'll be glad when we don't have to sneak around anymore, or don't have to lie to Syn. Where is Steel?"

"He had to run out. He received a link from Captain Maynard saying he needed to see him right away. Something about some information that Steel was trying to get for someone. He said not to worry, that he wouldn't be gone long."

I don't know why, but I get a cold chill. Maybe he found out something about Douglas. Before I can raise any concerns, everyone bursts into the kitchen pouncing all over Ady. They're all so excited about the baby.

My link goes off and it's Kell. *"Hey beautiful, what time do you want me there to meet your family? I'm glad we're finally telling Syn."*

"Me too. Come over in about two hours. I want a little time with them by myself first."

"I understand, but I can't wait to have some alone time with you. It's been a long busy week. I'm looking forward to touching you."

"I'm looking forward to you touching me," I whisper. "I'll see you in a couple hours.

"Dinner is ready, but Steel hasn't made it back yet." Ady looks a little concerned.

"I'll try his link," I say and leave her with mom and Aunt Brogan.

I walk into Steel's office for some privacy. "Steel?"

No response. "Steel?" I ask again. Nothing.

Syn walks in as he hears me trying to link. "What's wrong?"

"I don't know, Steel should be back by now and he's not answering his link. He went to see Captain Maynard about something. I'm worried."

"Let me try the captain's link." He walks over to the window and links with him. When he turns back around his face is pale.

"What is it?" I walk his direction.

"He said he was still waiting on Steel to show up."

I frantically try his link again. "Steel, where are you?" Nothing, not even static.

"What am I missing, Gray? What haven't you told me?"

"He was looking into something for me."

"What, Gray?" he demands.

"I met Steel for lunch the other day. Before I got there, Douglas Davis happened to be there and introduced himself to Steel as my friend. I told him that I didn't have a good feeling about it and he offered to check him out. Ady said that Captain Maynard called and had some information for him."

"And you think it was about Douglas?"

"Maybe. Why would Steel not answer his link unless there was something wrong?"

He tries his link with Steel and he doesn't get an answer either.

"Hey, you two, dinner is getting cold. I'm sure Steel will be here any minute." Ady says as she walks into the room.

Syn and I glance at each other.

"What are you two up to?" she asks placing her hands on her hips.

"Um...Captain Maynard hasn't seen Steel yet." I walk up to her and touch her arm. Syn is right behind me.

"He left hours ago. Didn't you try his link?" She looks alarmed.

"Yes, he's not answering."

"That's not like him, he always answers. Unless something's happened to him. " I see her hand touch her belly.

"I'll get back on the link with Captain Maynard, and have him locate Steel's tracker." He steps out of the room.

"Come on. Let's go into the living room with the rest of the family. I'm sure Syn will find him."

When we walk into the living room, everyone immediately knows there's something wrong when they see Ady's face.

"Steel is missing." She lets out a sob.

Everyone jumps to their feet and rushes to her side surrounding her. "Syn is trying to locate him now, he's not answering his link."

"Is there any reason to think that Steel is in danger?" Kyren asks with concern.

I tell them about our run-ins with Douglas. That I'm sure it's nothing, but my gut tells me different.

"You should always trust your gut," my dad adds." I hear Ady whimper.

The gate monitor goes off and I know Kell is here. I can't stop any of this now.

Steel's missing, no one has seen him for hours. There's info I don't know about Douglas, important enough that Steel left his pregnant wife to go get it. And Ady is an emotional wreck now. The two people I needed to deal with Syn and Kell can't help me. I'm really worried about Steel. I can't talk to Syn with him missing.

I walk over and push the button to let Kell through the gate. I wait at the door for him to pull up so I can meet him at his Hummer.

"I'm sorry you've driven over here, I should have linked to you to cancel."

He climbs out. "Why, what's wrong?" His hands hold me at arm's length.

"Steel is missing." As I get the words out, I hear Syn's thunderous voice behind me.

"What the hell are you doing here?" He storms between us.

"I guess you didn't get the chance to tell him." Kell inhales.

"Tell me what?" Syn turns to me angry.

"I—"

"What's all the yelling about?" I hear my dad. I turn around and everyone is standing behind me. Aunt Brogan comes up beside me and holds my hand. Right now, she is suddenly my lifeline.

We both turn to face Syn again. "Kell and I have been seeing one another for a while now." I swallow hard waiting for his wrath.

He steps closer to me. "Why am I just now hearing about it?" he asks between gritted teeth.

"I knew you'd stop it and send him away." I step closer to whisper in his ear. "Kell doesn't remember anything. Please, be mad at me. Don't say anything else in front of him." I'm pleading with him.

Kell comes over to us. "I don't understand the problem, Syn. I love your cousin and I promise it won't interfere with our working relationship or our friendship."

My eyes are locked with Syn's. I silently implore him. He closes his eyes tight before he turns to face Kell. "I can't get into this with the two of you right now. My priority is finding Steel." He stomps back into the house.

"I'm so sorry about all of this," I tell Kell.

"He's right, we need to find Steel," he says matter-of-factly. "I'm a detective, so's Syn, and we work well together. Let me help. Syn's too close to this."

I really don't want him in this any deeper. "I think maybe you should just go home."

He hangs his head. I can't tell if he's offended, defeated, or hurt.

"Well, I think he should stay and help," Aunt Brogan offers. I turn to look at her surprised by her words. She leans into my ear to whisper, "He's going to know the truth eventually, at least let it happen while we're all here to help both of you." I squeeze her hand, then grab Kell's and introduce him to my family.

As we all walk back in, I pull Ady to the side. "Any word yet?"

"No. The captain was having some issue with his computer at home, so he was driving to his office to use the computer there. Syn is waiting for him to link back."

"What can I do to help?" Kell is by my side.

"We're waiting to hear back on his locator."

Syn walks back in and everyone is completely silent. "His locator shows him at an abandoned warehouse twenty miles from here."

Ady gasps. "I'm going with you."

"No, you're not. You're five or six months pregnant. Steel would not want you in danger. I have no idea what I will be walking into."

"What WE will be walking into," Kell argues. "We're partners, you're not going in by yourself."

"No, he's not going alone. But you're not going either, Kell. I'll go with him." I state flatly.

"You're not trained to help in a situation like this, but I am," Kell insists. He doesn't know I'm a trained sniper. I made sure to never tell him about my military history.

I chuckle. "You have no idea what I'm capable of doing."

Everyone starts talking at the same time and Syn whistles loudly to get their attention. "I'll take Gray and Kyren with me," he commands.Kyren nods in agreement.

"If Gray is going, then I'm going, too." Kell looks fierce.

"Suit yourself," Syn says gruffly. "Let's get armed and ready." He leads us to Steel's stock room and starts pulling out vests, guns, rifles and military gear.

I take the rifle and start checking it. "You know how to use that?" Kell asks with a frown on his brow. He's staring hard at me holding a rifle. I can't worry about it now, not with Steel in obvious danger.

"Trust me, I know how to use it," I say absently, as I rapidly test that everything seems in good working order. I quickly attach the scope and reach for a silencer to pocket. I grab two extra clips, make sure they're loaded and walk past him.

"I'll have the computer link up, please let me know as soon as you find him." Ady cries and is surrounded by the rest of the family.

"Try not to worry. We'll find him and bring him back." I briefly hug her and we head out the door and load up in my Jeep. I pray we find him and it's not too late.

Kell's not saying anything, but I can't worry about it right now. I really wish Syn had refused to let him come. That feeling in my gut about Douglas, it feels like I've been punched now. I soldier on. I have to.

CHAPTER

1 made the mistake of sitting in the back seat. Syn's eyes keep cutting into me in the rearview mirror. I can see by his tensed jawline that he's holding back some serious rage. Kyren finally breaks the silence.

"Why would this Douglas guy want to hurt Steel?"

"I honestly have no idea," I say.

"He doesn't." Syn snaps.

"So, you still think it's a coincidence? I told you something was up with him. You didn't believe me then, and as soon as Steel starts investigating him he's missing!" I yell back at him.

Kell grabs my hand. "Who's this Douglas guy? And what connection does he have to Steel?"

How do I tell him without giving anything away? Now is not the time to clue him in.

"He had a twin brother that was in the military and he died," Syn states empathetically.

"What does that have to do with Steel?" Kell asks again. It's the detective in him, to ask questions.

"Grief is a powerful motivator, maybe he relates Steel with his brother." I know Syn is reaching with his answers and I'm still not sure he even believes that Douglas has anything to do with it.

"You two need to come clean right now with everything that you know," Kyren says fuming. He's in the dark as much as Kell.

"Look, rather than jumping to wild conclusions, why don't we wait and see if Steel is even in trouble. Maybe he's running an errand and needed to keep it a secret." Syn says.

Kyren grabs the steering wheel and jerks it off the road and Syn slams on the brakes sending us all flying forward.

"Stop the bullshit! I can tell you're not telling us everything. Tell me right now!" I have never seen Uncle Kyren so mad.

"Okay, okay." Syn puts his hands up in surrender. "Our last mission was a rescue as you know."

Kell interrupts. "You and Steel?"

"No." I barely whisper. "I was on a mission with Syn."

"I don't understand." He squeezes my hand.

"We rescued two soldiers that'd been held captive. One survived and one didn't. The one that died was Douglas's twin brother. He may be holding a grudge and taking it out on Steel," Syn answers him.

"So, you think because his brother wasn't brought back alive that he wants your brother dead?" Kyren's teeth are gritted.

"That is my assumption." I didn't realize that Syn and I were thinking the same thing. "I think he was researching us. Watching us and waited for an opportunity to take Steel." Syn says.

"Why not take the soldier that survived?" Kell asks. "Where is that guy at? Maybe someone should check on him. He could be in danger too."

Oh hell. Can we please stop talking? Let me shoot something.

Syn turns in his seat to face Kell. I lean forward and fiercely lock eyes with him.He opens his mouth to say something and I can tell he changed his mind about what he was going to say by his hesitation.

"I already have, Kell. And I'm certain he's safe. I know exactly where he is. This isn't about him. This Douglas must want a brother for brother. I led the mission, his brother died. Now, he's taken my brother."

"Then, we're wasting time just sitting here," Kyren states. "Let's get going!"

Syn turns around and drives back out on the dark road.

"I didn't know you were in the military," Kell sits looking at me. "Why didn't you tell me?"

"It's not a time in my life that I like to talk about, but when we get through this, I will tell you everything." His eyes change and he shifts in his seat uncomfortably and rubs his furrowed brow.

"I somehow knew you then, didn't I? I keep having faded visions of you on a rooftop and you had a rifle in your hand. I think something bad happened, too." He's shutting his eyes and rubbing his brow harder.

We ride another thirty minutes in complete silence before Syn pulls the car over. "We're here." We all jump out of the Jeep and dig our gear out of the back. It's pitch black outside, with a layer of fog that makes it even harder to see.

"I don't see a warehouse," Kyren comments looking around.

"No, you don't," Syn answers. "That's the whole point of stopping here. It's about a quarter of a mile up the road. I didn't want anyone to see or hear us coming," Syn states, as he points in the direction we need to go. "Gray, you take off in front of us and get set up." I'm now in military mode and don't pay any attention to Kell's immediate protests. I know that Syn will reign him in.

I take off running through the darkness relying solely on Syn's directions. It doesn't take long before the warehouse is in view. I approach the target in a running crouch. It's all dark, except one dimly lit area in the back. I sneak around to try and get a glimpse into the broken window. I find an old cracked milk crate and carefully stand on it to look inside. I see three cages off in a corner and Steel is laying lifeless inside one of them. I stumble from the wobbly crate and land flat on my ass. At least I did it quietly.

"Syn, I see him. He's locked in a cage and he's not moving. I'm going inside."

"You'll do as you're told. Get somewhere you can set up like I ordered. We'll be there in less than a minute. You're covering us."

I flash my light around the grounds and I see an area on a hill that'll give me a near perfect advantage point with my lighted scope. I take off running and see Syn, Kell, and Kyren coming around the corner. Syn points and the three of them disperse around the warehouse, staying close to the metal walls.

"Are you in place, Gray?"

"Yes. I'm on the hilltop. He's in the back of the warehouse. I don't see anyone else inside with him."

"Stay in place until I tell you to move," Syn orders.

Our link is joined with Kell. Kyren was also given an earpiece to connect. I hear Syn order them to move inside.

I don't see any movement or shifts of light in the room that Steel is being held. I know to be silent, but it's damn near killing me, then the silence is broken by gunfire.

I still don't see any movement. "Syn... Kell..."

More shots are fired. "Syn, answer me!" I'm up and running.

"Don't come in here yet." I finally hear Syn and he sounds like he's in pain. I stop dead in my tracks.

"Tell me what's going on?"

"My dad has been captured. I've been shot in the leg. I don't know where Kell is."

I start to say something and then I hear a voice come over a loudspeaker.

159

Kelly Moore

"I knew you all would join me sooner or later. I've waited patiently for you for a long time." The voice sounds distorted, punctuated by crackles and a background hiss.

"What do you want from us?" Syn yells at him.

"I want you to pay for my brother's life. You saved yours, but left mine to die."

"We didn't leave him, we found him. We didn't kill him, he was barely breathing when we reached him. We tried to save him, but he was too far gone. The men that tortured him killed him. We're not your enemy, they are. Stand down. No one else has to die," Syn tries to reason with him.

"I've done my research. You brought back your cousin's lover. You chose to save him and not my brother. Now where is that selfish bitch? Tell her to show her whore face!"

I'm unbothered by his words. ""Syn, I'm coming in."

"Not yet. Don't give him the upper hand. See if you can find him." Syn orders.

"Have you seen Kell? Can you see Kyren?"

"Not yet. The lights just went out. I can hear movement. It sounds like someone is being dragged across the floor."

"I'm on the move. I'm going to go in the door that I saw Kell enter."

"Be careful, don't show your face."

I make my way through the dark to the back entrance and quietly open the door and hit the floor in a sniper crawl. I can only move a few inches at a time because it's so dark.

I stop as I hear footsteps and hold my breath to not make a sound. A few seconds later, I hear the footsteps going the opposite way. The loud speaker comes on again and I see a light flicker from under a door on the far side of the room.

*"**Well, whoever we have here is a bonus!**"* Douglas laughs.

He must be wearing a wireless microphone connected to the loudspeakers.

"What's he talking about Syn, can you see anything?" I whisper.

"My dad is in one of the cages. He's alive because I can see him moving. Any sign of Kell?"

"No, but there must be more than one of them. I heard footsteps right before the speaker came on. Are you out of sight?"

"I'm sure if they'd have seen me, I'd be in a cage by now."

"How bad is your leg?"

"I've got the bleeding stopped, but it hurts like a motherfucker."

"Are you still armed?"

"No. My gun slid under a container when I got hit. I can't reach it without being seen."

*"**Are you going to tell me where Gray is or not?**"* Douglas yells into the mic.

"I need to find out where he is and take him out." I move slowly again.

"I can see a set of stairs on the east side of the room. I'm betting that's where he's hiding," Syn whispers.

*"**If you don't show your face and answer me soon, I'll have to order my men to kill whoever your friend is here that we've captured.**"*

161

I see two men come out of nowhere, holding guns. They look like military.

"I'm coming out, Gray. You and Kell are still our advantage. I can't let them kill my dad."
"I'm headed your way."

I hear Syn yell to not shoot, that he's coming out unarmed.

"That leaves you, princess. I know you're here, too." Douglas taunts me.

"Kell, where the hell are you?"
"I'm in the..." The link goes dead.
"Shit." I continue my crawl and I see the light go out again.

"Come out, come out, wherever you are, princess." He taunts again.

I'm going to kill him. I hear footsteps again. I manage to get behind a door just as it opens. I hear the click of a gun right before I see a light sweep through the room. Whoever it is, doesn't step any further inside and I remain stock still behind the door.

"I'm going to give you to the count of ten. If you don't show your face, I'm going to start killing them one by one.I think I'll start with the soon never to be papa."

I hear a gut wrenching scream and know that it's Kell. Did they get him too? How many more of these damn guys are there?

As soon as the door closes, I'm up on my feet. I use the element of surprise in my favor. The lights come back on and I hear "*one, two...*"

I burst through the door and immediately take out the one that has a gun pointed at Kell's head. Then I turn and shoot the other two men in my sight. I duck behind a container to refocus around the room. The mic sounds like it is being dropped and it's blessedly silent again.

Syn yells out to me, "Up the stairs!"

I take off in a full run. As I'm moving up the stairs, I hear Syn link with 911. I hear a crash coming from behind the door. I kick open the door and I see Douglas climbing out the window that he broke with an old metal folding chair that is laying sideways on the floor.

"Stop!" I yell. He lets go of the ledge as soon as the words come out of my mouth. I race over to the window crunching the broken glass under my feet. I look out the window cautiosly, and I can barely see him getting up and running off into the woods. It's too foggy for me to get a clear shot at him.

I race back downstairs to see Kell, frozen in place staring at the cages. Kyren's cage is unlocked I check on him first.

"Are you okay?" I ask, touching him to find injuries. There's blood coming out from under his right arm.

"I took a hit in the gap of my vest under my arm."

"Let me see." I turn him to look. "You need to hold pressure right here." I take his hand and place it where it needs to be. "Can you do that?"

"I'm fine, go check on Steel."

"Kell, I need your help getting these cages open." He doesn't move or respond.

"Kell! Damnit, I need your help!" He just blinks. I shoot the lock off Syn's cage and then Steel's. "Help me, Syn!" I point to him.

I crawl inside Steel's cage. "Steel, can you hear me?" I check for a pulse, it's faint. I start looking for injuries. I see needle track lines on his left arm. I recognize them from my own captivity. "Shit, they've drugged him."

"An ambulance is on its way," Syn barks out.

I remove his vest and shirt to see if there are any other injuries I don't know about. He had to put up a hell of a fight, even unarmed. I gasp when I see his chest. It's purple and black where he's been beaten.

"What is it?" Syn barks.

"It's bad. I think he has internal injuries. The assholes beat him with something." I hear a gurgling noise come from deep in his throat and I feel for a pulse again. It's gone.

No. I can't lose him. Ady and her child need him. I start CPR. "I need help in here! Kell, get in here!" He's sitting in Syn's cage staring at me. He'd even closed the cage door behind him. "Now, Kell!" He doesn't budge or seem to hear me.

Kyren stumbles to his feet, carefully holding his arm. He ignores his pain and staggers his way into to cage to help me with Steel. I keep doing compressions and Kyren starts giving him rescue breaths.

Syn is dragging himself out of his cage and yelling at Kell to help me.

I watch Kell curl into a ball like he did when we first found him in his prison. My heart is breaking for him, but I have to focus on what I'm doing.

"Don't you die on me, you son of a bitch!" Syn is yelling at Steel.

"See if he has a pulse yet." I direct Syn.

He places his fingers on his jugular as I pause compressions. "Nothing." His voice cracks.I resume my relentless pounding on Steel's already injured chest, I can feel his ribs cracking beneath my hands. I have no idea if I am doing more damage.

"Come on, Son!" Kyren cries out, between breaths.

"I hear sirens," Syn says and gets on his link with the dispatcher directing them exactly where we are in the warehouse and that our captor escaped into the woods.

A few seconds later a military and medical team rush through the doors. They take over CPR and hook Steel up to their equipment. I fall back onto my knees as they take him out of the cage.

Syn is telling the military police squad about Douglas. They immediately send out a scout team with dogs to find him.

I help Kyren up before pulling Syn to his feet while supporting his weight. We stand out of the way and watch them continue to work on Steel for what seems like hours that were actually only minutes.

"Anything yet?" I ask one of the medics.

He shakes his head. "We're getting our hypothermia unit ready to place him into until we get him to the hospital."

We can do nothing but watch as they bring in their unit and place Steel inside and shut the cover. As they are taking him out, the military unit comes in the door, but Douglas isn't with them. I wish I'd shot the bastard.

"The dogs followed his trail, but lost it in the river," one of the soldiers tells Syn.

Two other medics start working on Syn and Kyren. I glance over and Kell is still in a fetal position in the cage. I cautiously walk over to him.

"Kell," I say his name softly. He doesn't move. He doesn't respond.

"I'm staying behind with them," Syn tells the medic.

"Sir, we really need to get you to the hospital to work on your leg."

"It was a clean shot all the way through. The bleeding has stopped. I'll stay here and help them. Take my dad to the hospital with my brother. We'll catch up."

"It's okay, Syn. Go with them," I tell him. "You can't walk back to the car on that leg."

"I'm not leaving you here with him alone. Not when I don't know where his mind is right now." His words come out tender, not angry.

"You need to be with your brother and father. Ady is going to need you there. I'll take care of Kell and then meet you at the hospital. Get yourself patched up, I can't drag both of you a quarter of a mile."

"The MPs were going to give us a lift," he starts to argue. He winces as he puts weight on his leg. Reluctantly, he concedes and goes off with the medics, leaning on one of them for support.

I know he hates leaving anyone behind.

CHAPTER 18

"Kell?" I crawl into the cage and place my hand gently on his shoulder. "Kell, I need to know if you can hear me?"

His eyes slightly open. I lay down beside him so that I can look at him directly in the eyes. "Talk to me." I search his dark eyes for understanding.

It takes a moment, but he finally speaks. "I was that other soldier. I was the one you saved. I remembered as soon as he started counting. This was about me. I'm the cause of this." He's barely speaking above a whisper, as blood drips down his forehead.

"You've been injured. Let me look at your head."

"No." He rolls to his back and rubs the blood from his face. "You were there, too."

"Yes."

"How come I didn't remember? How could I not have known that you were a sniper and that I loved you?"

"I think you did remember that you loved me, that's how we ended up together again."

He sits up abruptly and I join him. "What did they do to me?" He looks angry. "What's wrong with me? It's like all of you know something and you aren't telling. I saw the stare down you had with your cousin, in the car. He was about to say something. You stopped him, I think."

He's putting it together, my lover, the detective. Only he doesn't have all the pieces to the puzzle.

"When we found you, you were in really bad shape. We brought you back here to the hospital, but you refused help. You wanted to die. You didn't want anything to do with me either." I pause and wait for any reaction.

He doesn't move or say anything, he just starts rubbing his forehead again. He doesn't notice he's smearing blood.

"The doctors said that you'd never be the same. You refused to eat or take your medications. You thought they were trying to kill you. They suggested... drastic measures. They kept pushing for a decision. I made the decision to let them erase your memory and place new one's in your mind." A tear falls down my face. He reaches over and wipes it away.

"It was the hardest decision that I ever had to make because it meant that I had to lose you all over again to save you. They said that I couldn't be part of your life or your memory might come back. I was devastated. Syn agreed to be your handler so that I'd always know that you were okay. We weren't ever supposed to see each other again." My tears fall freely.

"The moment I first laid eyes on you in the restaurant, deep down I knew you. Pieces of you kept popping into my head" He looks around the room. "I thought you were dead. They told me that they killed you because you were pregnant." His breath hitches. "I wanted to die that night. I wish you'd have just let them kill me that day you were on the roof." He turns to face me. "Were you really even pregnant? Did they lie about that too?" His eyes are filled with tears.

"Yes. I lost the baby when they beat me. A butcher made sure that I'd never get pregnant again. I wanted to die that day, too. They killed our baby." My tears fall harder.

He crawls out of the cage and starts walking in circles with his hands on his head. All of a sudden, he lets out a gut-wrenching scream. He picks up a cage and throws it across the room. I quickly get out and stand out of his way. He continues picking up each cage and slinging them through the room. He picks up my rifle by the barrel and beats it on the floor until it's in pieces. I don't try to stop him.

I can do nothing but watch his pain explode. He takes his rage out on boxes that are stacked. By the time he's done, there's nothing left standing in the room. I'm aware that this was a crime scene. We'll just have to deal with it later. His chest is heaving and his hands are grasped into fists. I'm not frightened of him, but I'm frightened for him. I'm surprised none of the MPs came in to check.

"Kell...I'm...I'm sorry. I never would've left if I knew you were alive. They'd have had to kill me before I ever would've left you. I just didn't know. I'm so sorry."

He calms his breathing and walks up to me. He pulls me close and holds me tight to his chest. "You have nothing to be sorry for, I'm glad you got out when you did. It killed me every minute that you were there and I couldn't protect you. It was my fucking job to protect you." He's sobbing as he goes to his knees wrenched over in pain.

I rub my hands through his hair. "Baby, it was out of both of our control. They were savages. I wanted to protect you, too." I slide to my knees and let him cry. He raises up and holds me to him again like I'm his lifeline.

"Are you okay?" I ask.

"I honestly don't know. There are so many things that I need to process."

"Can I take you to the hospital? Your doctor needs to see you and I think you need a couple of stitches in your head."

"I'll go, but you need to go check on your family while I'm seeing the doctor." He stands with me and glances around the room one more time. "I hate this place almost as much as I hated my cage."

As soon as we get on the road I link with Syn. "How is Steel?"

"Not good. He's in surgery. They've coded him twice more already."

"Where's Ady?"

"My mom and your parents are on their way with her. They took the bullet out of my dad. He'll be fine."

"And you?"

"There wasn't much for them to do other than clean it out and stitch me up. How is Kell?"

I glance over at him. "That's hard to answer. At least he's agreed to come to the hospital to see his doctor. We'll be there in about thirty minutes or so."

I disconnect and keep glancing at Kell. He's eerily quiet again, after his previous outrage. I reach over to hold his hand, but his stare remains fixed out the window. I wish I knew what he was thinking. I don't want to push him. "I love you. I've always loved you."

He squeezes my hand but says nothing.

I take Kell's hand and lead him to the nurse's station, where his doctor is waiting for us. Syn called him to let him know we were coming.

He greets Kell, who still has not spoken since we left the warehouse or the entire drive here. I search his eyes. He looks lost and the light in them has dulled.

"I need to go check on Steel. I'll come back after the doctor has examined you." I see a slight nod of his head. I hate to leave him now, but I need to see my family.

I run up the flights of stairs. The small waiting room is overflowing with my family where they are all surrounding Ady. Mom and dad see me first and rush over to hug me.

"How is he?"

"We still don't know anything yet," Dad answers.

I leave the comfort of their arms and go to Ady. "I'm so sorry," is all I can say as I hug her to me.

"Syn said you got to him as soon as you could and started CPR," she sobs. "I can't lose him," she cries even harder.

"You're not going to lose him, the two of you have been through too much already. I know he'll fight with everything he has in him just to come back to you. You have to believe that." I have to believe that. I feel responsible for all of this. I should have trusted my gut and none of this would have happened.

Ady calms down a little and sits back between Aunt Brogan and my mom. "How is Uncle Kyren?"

"I just left him. His surgery went fine, but he was ripping everything out to get to Steel. I had the doctor give him something stronger to calm him down and he's asleep right now. How is Kell?" she asks, truly concerned.

"I don't know. I left him to come up here to be with all of you. He's with his doctor and I know he is at least physically safe." I turn to look for Syn and he is standing down the hallway looking out a window with his hands tucked in his pockets. I need to know that he's okay, too.

I walk up and stand beside him and remove his hand from his pocket and take it in mine. "Why are you down here by yourself and not with our family?"

"I'm so fucking scared, I can't sit in there with them." I hear his voice catch and it scares the hell out of me. I've never heard Syn admit to being scared of anything. "This is all my fault. I'm a detective. When you told me something wasn't right with Douglas, I should have done some digging. I was so distracted by other

171

things that I let it slip. I should have trusted you. You were right. This is my fault."

"At this point, the only person we can blame is Douglas. He wanted revenge for something he believed was our fault and I don't think any of us could have stopped him."

"What if he doesn't make it?" Tears are streaming down his face.

I hear my dad's voice behind me. "Syn, Gray...the doctor is coming out to update us."

We both quickly return to the waiting room just as the surgeon enters. Brogan steadies Ady and walks her to him. "How is my husband?"

"There was a tear in his aorta that caused his heart to stop and he had massive amounts of blood loss. We were able to repair the tear and transfuse him. Starting CPR in the field and placing him in hypothermia bought him some extra time. He would have surely died if not for that. But, he's still in grave condition. I've placed him back into to the hypothermia chamber. He needs time to see if his body can recover from this."

Ady's knees give and Syn catches her. "How long?" Aunt Brogan asks him.

"I honestly don't know. We can keep him in the chamber for months if we need to and he will be monitored hourly. We've had some remarkable outcomes with hypothermia treatments."

"Is he in pain?" Ady sobs.

"No, we will keep him very comfortable. As soon as his vitals stabilize without intervention, we will wake him up. I'm sorry that I can't give you a definite time frame on when and if that is going to happen."

"Can we see him?" Syn asks.

"In about an hour, we will have him set up in his ICU room and you can see him then."

"Thank you for saving him." Ady sobs again.

"We're doing everything we can for him, Mrs. Nolan." He turns and heads back into the operating room.

"While we wait, I'm going to check back in on Kyren. Then we'll get you something to eat," Aunt Brogan says to Ady.

"I'm not hungry. I just want to sit here until I can see him." She sits back down.

"Of course. But, you also have to take care of yourself and the baby," Aunt Brogan insists. "We can bring you something."

Tears fall again as she rubs her belly. "He has to make it to meet this little one."

"My son will fight to live for you and this baby. You need to fight on your end to make sure you and this baby are healthy and strong when he opens his eyes."

Mom stops and turns to hug me again. "What can I do for you?"

"You're already doing it, Mom." I let her hold me to her. Dad joins in and we cry with each other for a moment. "I need to go check on Kell," I say as I step out of their arms.

"Do you want us to go with you?" Dad asks.

"I'll go with her," I hear Syn say from behind me. He shrugs, "I'm still his handler."

That's not really why. He cares about Kell.

We take the stairs instead of the elevator, neither one of us speaking. A nurse stops us before we enter Kell's room. "The doctor wants to see you in his office before you go in there."

My heart starts racing. Things are bad enough with Steel, I don't think I can handle any more bad news. She leads us into his office and he shakes hands with Syn.

"Please, have a seat." He points to two cushioned chairs in the corner of his bright office.

"After you left here, Kell broke down. We had to sedate him. He tried to leave and grabbed one of our security guards by the throat. He thought he was a Chinese soldier. We were able to sedate him before he hurt anyone or hurt himself."

I feel all the air leave my lungs and is replaced with pain. My hand automatically goes to my mouth. "This is all my fault. I should have stayed away from him." Syn holds my hand and squeezes it.

"What do you think will happen to him when he wakes up?" Syn asks.

"By my assessment of him, I'm afraid we're right back to where we were before we erased his memory. I think him seeing those cages, the added stress of seeing people get hurt, it released all his repressed memories of his time in being imprisoned in them. It was too much for his mind to overcome. I'm afraid our only choice is to erase his memory again, but this time he should have no contact with any of you and he should remain in one of our facilities."

"You want to keep him locked up? I'll stay away from him, just please don't lock him up again!" I yell as I stand.

I've only brought him from one prison to another. I suddenly feel very hot and the room is spinning. I don't know how much more I can handle in one day.

Syn is up and on his feet trying to calm me down. "You don't look so good, please sit back down."

I feel a wave of nausea roll over me. I make it to the garbage can just in time. Syn is holding my hair back and talking quietly to me. My mind is all over the place and I have no idea what he is saying to me. All I know is that I will lose Kell again and my cousin may not survive. I'm only human. I can only handle so much.

This is it...

This is my breaking point...

I can't take any more...

I want to stop breathing...

I want to stop hurting...

I want to forget...

I feel like there's a knife stabbing me in the heart and I can't take anymore. "Please, just get me out of here," I plead with Syn.

He helps me up off the ground and holds me around the waist as we leave the office. I can't help but glance back at Kell's room. "Please, let me say goodbye to him," I whisper to Syn.

He walks me over to the door and a security guard stops us.

"Let them in," the doctor intervenes.

Kell's eyes are closed and he looks pained even in his sleep. I rub the scowl in his brow hoping to comfort him. "I love you. I'm so sorry that I put you through this again. All I have ever wanted is you." I start to cry. "I promise I'll let you go this time, but please try to find some happiness, someone that loves you like I do. I can't stand the thought of a man like you being alone." I bend down and kiss his cheek. "Goodbye, Kell."

"Do you want me to take you back upstairs to see Steel?" Syn asks.

"No, I really want to go home. You stay, I can drive myself."

"You're in no condition to be alone right now, I'll take you."

"But..."

"But nothing. I'm staying with you."

It makes me wonder if he heard my thoughts. I know he should stay here, but I'm glad he's not leaving me. I've always been so strong, but this is more than I can handle right now. "Okay."

CHAPTER

My parents have moved into my house. I haven't been out of bed in three days. Cy hasn't left my side. Every part of me aches. I'm afraid that if I leave the comfort of my own bed, something else bad will happen. My parents have built a pallet on the floor next to me. The first night here, mom curled up in bed with me a rocked me like she did when I was a child. I cried myself to sleep for the last time. I'm all cried out, there are no more tears, only emptiness remains.

Syn has come by every day to tell us that there have been no changes with Steel. Ady hasn't left his side. He's tried to find out about Kell, but the doctor is no longer giving us any information about him. Even Aunt Brogan tried, but with no luck. Syn's parents haven't left the hospital either. Kyren has been released but refuses to leave.

"Time to get your ass out of that bed, Gray," Syn growls as he pulls the covers off of me.

"Go away, Syn. Leave me alone." I pull the covers back up.

"Not a chance." This time he grabs me by the feet and pulls me to the floor and I bounce hard.

"Damn it, Syn! Leave me alone!" I yell again.

He throws clothes at me. "Get up and get dressed. I've got news and you need to go see Ady."

My heart stops. "Did something happen to Steel?" I scramble for the clothes he threw at me.

"Come out here when you're dressed! But do us all a favor and get a shower first!" He finishes yelling and slams the door behind him.

I take a quick glance in the mirror and I do look horrible. I quickly shower and dress. Mom, dad, and Syn are all sitting at the dining room table.

"Hey, angel." My Dad says as he sees me. He pulls out a chair for me to sit next to him.

"What's happened?" I say wasting no time.

"Steel is the same." He hesitates, "You were completely right about Douglas. We found information on his computer that proves he was researching us. He had laid out a plan to kill all of us. He was so angry about his twin that he couldn't get past it. He blamed us for his brother's death."

"He followed Steel once he left here that night. He had let the air out of one of Steel's tires. When he got out to fix it, Douglas snuck up on him and jabbed heroin into his neck. He put Steel into his car and took him to the warehouse that he and his buddies had set up. As one of them was putting Steel into the cage, he woke up and started fighting with them. One of them picked up a steal beam and hit him several times in the chest. If that wasn't enough, they put some more heroin in his veins to keep him knocked out."

"He knew we'd track him, but he didn't count on Dad being there or Kell. He knew you'd have your rifle and that's why he locked himself in the upstairs room with the mic. They haven't found the bastard yet, but when they do, he will be going to jail for a long time."

"I wish I could say that knowing this fixes things, but Steel is still on life support and god knows what's happening to Kell."

"I know you're hurting, but Ady needs you. You're her best friend and she could use your support," Mom says sweetly.

Kelly Moore

"You're right." I blow out a long breath. My mind needs to go into my military mode again and focus on what needs to be done and not pay attention to my heart. Maybe never.

"Good, we'll all go together." Dad stands.

When we're in the elevator at the hospital, I want to stop as we ride past Kell's floor. It takes everything in me not to push the stop button. The three of them sit in the waiting room as I go into the ICU. Ady is curled up in a chair with her hand on the unit that Steel is encased inside. There are all kinds of wires and monitors piped into the unit. The top is all see through glass. He looks so peaceful like he's simply sleeping.

"How is he today?" I ask quietly getting Ady's attention.

She pats the cushion next to her, gesturing for me to sit beside her. "I think he's a little stronger every day."

"That's good. I'm so sorry that I haven't been here." I hug her.

"It's okay. I heard about Kell. You lost the man you love for the third time. I can't blame you for not being here."

"But you and Steel are my family. I should have been here. He would have expected me to be here for you."

"You're here now, and that's all that matters," she says, holding my hand.

If I hadn't sworn off crying, I'd be in tears for her kindness. Maybe I'm still all cried out."How are you and this little one doing?" I rub her baby bump. It's gotten bigger.

"He or she has been kicking me a lot lately." She rubs her tummy. "The baby probably misses Daddy's voice. Steel read to my belly every night." A tear slides down her face.

"Have the doctor's said anything new?"

"They're still having to give him medicines and nutrition through all these tubes to keep his vitals stable. They try every morning to wean them down. But as soon as they do, he starts to crash."

"He's not ready yet, that's all. He just needs more time. I know he won't leave you and this little one behind."

"I want to believe that. I talk to him all the time like he can hear me." She laughs.

"I know he can hear you."

"Any word on Kell?"

"No, it's like he fell off the face of the earth. I don't even know if he's still here or if they've moved him. I can't get any information on him. They completely shut me out."

"That's terrible," she says as she stands up. "I have an idea, come with me."

I don't ask, I just follow. We slink by the waiting room and take the stairs down to Kell's floor. Before she opens the stairwell door she peeks through the glass. "Which room is his?"

"Why, what are you thinking?" I frown.

"I'm going to distract the guard and the nurses so that you can get inside to see him."

"I don't know, Ady. I promised that I'd leave him alone." I start pacing in the small space.

"Well, that was before they decided not to tell you anything about him. Weren't you designated to makes decisions for his medical issues, since he had no family? I remembered hearing that."

"That got revoked." I wring my hands together. "I really do want to make sure he's okay."

"Stay here and follow my lead," she says as she pushes through the door. I watch her as she goes to the nurse's station. I hear her scream out in pain and bend over holding her stomach. She's so believable, with her big stomach, I have to stop myself from running in to help her. It's working, too...the nurses come around to help her and even the guard is holding her up. My path is clear as if a bulldozer had gone though. I go to push through the door and I feel a hand grasp my shoulder.

"What the hell are you two doing?" Syn barks. "I knew you were up to no good when the two of you walked by the waiting room."

"Please, Syn. Let me go. I just need to make sure he's okay. I have to know. I promise that I'll come right back out. I won't even talk to him."

"I know that I'm going to regret this," he snarls and pushes the door open for me. He keeps watch at the door, standing inside the room with the door barely cracked.

I quickly make my way to Kell's room as they continue to help Ady. I open the door and the room is completely empty. No sheets are even on the bed. He's gone and I have no idea where he is and I can feel my heart fall.

"Excuse me, Miss. You don't belong in here." A guard pulls me out by the arm. Ady is being wheeled out on a gurney and Syn comes charging through the door.

"I will handle this." He takes me out of the guard's grasp. "I told you to never come here again," he snaps as he pushes me into the elevator and the doors close behind us.

"He's gone," I whisper.

All the feigned anger leaves his face. "I'm sorry," he says before he chuckles.

"What's so funny?" I ask scowling.

"We need to go rescue Ady before they admit her or even worse, sedate her to deliver a baby that's not ready yet. I swear I can't let the two of you out of my sight."

For one sweet moment, I let myself laugh.

Syn scolds both of us, but I can tell he's really not angry. He leaves us in Steel's room making us promise not to come up with any more schemes.

"It felt good to laugh for a minute. By the way, you are a good actress, I thought you were really in labor."

She laughs. "Glad I could help."

Then a deep sadness sets over me. "He's really gone this time."

"I'm so sorry. I could tell how much you loved him every time you mentioned his name. I know it's not much, but we will all be here for you."

I can't believe that with Steel laying here in front of us, not knowing whether he is going to make it or not, that she still shows so much compassion for me. A whole lot of this is my fault.

"Right now, the only thing we need to think about is Steel, and keeping you and this little one healthy."

CHAPTER

It's been weeks since I've heard anything or even seen Kell. I can't help but want to know where he is, and how he is doing. I decide to go to his apartment to see if his things are still there. I know that Syn has had the office closed since our ordeal with Douglas, but he's in the office tonight. He has the door locked. I can still see him sitting at his desk through the glass door. I tentatively knock, knowing that I'll have to face his wrath.

He crosses the room and stands in front of the door shaking his head when he sees me.

"Come on, Syn. Let me in."

"Go away!" he yells from behind the door.

"Please, let me in. It's cold out here." I pull my jacket closed.

He huffs out a breath and finally unlocks the door. "What are you doing here—as if I need to even ask?" He turns around and walks back over to his desk and sits down.

"I want to see his apartment," I say and hang my head.

"Why are you putting yourself through this again? He's not there." He leans his elbows on his desk and rests his chin in his hands.

"I miss him and I want to see that he is really gone."

"You think you're going to find something that can lead you to him."

It's not a question, but a statement. "I don't know, maybe." I sit down across from him. "I know I lied to you before. I haven't had the chance to explain all of it to you yet, and I need to apologize for lying to you."

He sits back and his chair squeaks. "I know why you lied, you knew I'd put a stop to your relationship with Kell." His hands lock behind his head.

I'm quiet for a moment trying to think about what I want to say next to him.

"I'm angry with you for lying to me, but I also get it. I know how much you've always loved him and I know he's a good man. I miss him, too."

"I'm so sorry, Syn. I tried to ignore him, but I couldn't. He kept pushing, but I could have said no. I know I'm to blame for the way things turned out, but I still need to know that he's okay. More importantly, I'm sorry that I lied to you, you didn't deserve that from me."

"No, I didn't. You're right, I wouldn't have helped you. I would have moved him for the sake of the two of you. I don't know what you think you're going to find in his apartment, though."

"Probably nothing, but maybe some kind of closure."

He opens a desk drawer and takes out a set of keys. He throws them across the desk toward me. "It's the middle one." He gets up and heads to the front door.

"You're leaving?" I ask.

"I'm going across the street for a cup of coffee. I can't stay here and watch you do this to yourself." The door shuts behind him.

I take the stairs in the back of the office that lead up to Kell's apartment. I flip the hallway light on so that I can see the keyhole. I open the door, and a deep sadness hits me hard at the emptiness.

I find a lamp and turn it on. The room is very masculine with dark leathers and tan colors. There are no pictures on the wall, but I see one on a side table. I walk over and pick it up. It's a picture of me curled up sleeping in the treehouse. He took it without me ever knowing. It makes me smile remembering my time there with him. At least I was dressed.

I walk into his bedroom and open his closet. It's empty. The same thing with his drawers. I can't stop myself, I crawl into his bed and his scent still lingers. I hug his pillow to my face and breathe him in. God, I wish he was here.

I hear a door creak. I don't move, thinking it's my imagination. I curl further into a ball and I hear a footstep. "Syn?" I listen but don't hear anything. I get up and softly walk over to the bedroom door. "Syn, is that you?"

I take one step out and an arm comes around my head and a hand over my mouth. I bend over trying to break free. I stomp on a foot and throw an elbow to their stomach. The grip around me loosens, but I can't break free. I yell Syn's name to connect with my link.

"He can't help you this time."

I immediately recognize Douglas's voice. He shifts and I feel the butt of a gun being jammed into my ribs. "What is it you want from me?" I yell.

"What I want, is my twin brother back. Do you have any idea what it's like to be a twin? I swear to you that I could feel his pain. I knew the moment that he died. It was agony not being able to help him!" He spits out. His voice turns hateful toward me. "You could have helped him too, but you chose to save only your boyfriend instead."

"That's not true! We tried to save your brother. He was too far gone by the time we reached him."

"I don't believe you. I want to know where your fucking boyfriend is...so that I can kill him with my bare hands!" he snarls through gritted teeth.

"You already managed to kill him mentally. Did you even know that? What more do you want? I don't understand your need for revenge on him. He went through the same thing your brother did."

He pulls my hair and yanks my face toward him. "I don't care about him. He's a pawn. It's you and your cousin that I want to hurt. The two of you deserve to lose the people closest to you."

"I would have done anything to save your brother," I protest. He pushes me on the floor and I have to catch myself before my face slams into the floor.

"You're a lying bitch!" he screams as he points the gun toward the back of my head.

"Put the gun down, Douglas," Syn says from the doorway pointing his gun at him.

"I'll get a shot off before you can kill me. Your sweet little cousin will be dead first." His face is contorted with unholy rage.

"No one has to die here today. Lower your gun, and step away from her." Syn takes one step closer.

"You think I care if I die?" He laughs. "I died the day my brother did. He was the only person left in this world that I cared about and the two of you took him from me!" He spat back at Syn from across the room.

"She's already told you that he was too far gone. We tried to save him. I don't want to kill you." Syn doesn't waiver with his aim.

"Please, let us help you, Douglas. I know the pain your brother went through. I'm sure he wouldn't want you suffering along with him. We can get you the help you need." I start to stand, but his aim becomes firmer and I stay in place.

"You can't help me and I don't want your help!" he yells as he swings the gun around toward Syn.

I quickly tackle him to the floor, before Syn can shoot him. The gun flies from his hand and slides across the floor. He rolls on top of me and gets his hands around my throat. I try to fight him off, but he is too strong. Syn moves towards us and places his gun at the bastard's head.

"I will kill you if you don't let go of her," he says. I'm frantically shaking my head at Syn.

Douglas finally lets go and I gasp for air to return to my lungs. He stands up and faces Syn. "Please, don't kill him, Syn," I manage to beg between gulps of air. I don't want another person to die. He's suffered enough and he needs help. Syn keeps his gun aimed at him as he links with the police.

I get off the ground and stand next to Syn. "Douglas, I'm so sorry that you lost your brother. We're not to blame, though. His captors killed him, and he wasn't the only one. Blame them not us, we're not your enemy. Please, let us get you some help."

I see some of the desperation leave his eyes. He looks incredulous. "Why would you want to help me after what I've done to your family?"

"Because there's been enough loss for all of us. The war claimed enough lives. We don't need to add any more to it."

He slowly sits down on the couch behind him. And all I see is another broken man. His sobs fill the room. I sit down beside him, but I don't touch him. I'm not really sure what to do. What he's done to Steel is unforgivable. He needs to be punished, but I can't help but feel sorry for him.

Within a few minutes, the military police arrive and handcuff him. We follow them downstairs, and I watch as they place him in the back of their vehicle.

"He'll get the help he needs. And he'll be locked up for a long time," Syn says as he squeezes my shoulder.

My eyes are fixed on the car until it is no longer in sight. "Are you okay?" Syn asks.

"Sorry. The thought of anyone being locked up turns my stomach."

"He won't be mistreated like you were." He places his arm around me.

"Thanks for coming in when you did. Things could have ended very differently."

"I'm glad you had the sense to link with me. I ran out of the coffee shop not knowing what I would find when I reached you. I should have locked the door behind me."

"He must have been following me. I've been so out of my mind worried about Steel and Ady, that I haven't paid attention to my surroundings like I normally would." We walk toward my Jeep.

"Did you find what you needed in the apartment?" he asks.

"I found that he is really gone. The only thing he left behind was a picture of me. He probably left it because he had no idea who it was. I know I need to let him go once and for all. I need to focus on the good things in my life." I climb behind the wheel.

"Let me follow you home. I feel the need to be near my family tonight, anyway."

CHAPTER

21

I t's January and it's been a cold harsh winter for us. We've all taken turns sitting with Steel so that Ady could leave the hospital for a few hours each day. Her tummy has gotten big and she only has another month to go.

With all the stress that she has been under, the doctor has recommended bed rest for her, but she refuses. One of us is with her at all times; encouraging her to eat, sleep, and drink. She has been so strong through all of this, but you can tell it's starting to take its toll on her.

I've been with Steel all morning while the nurses take care of him, monitoring his vitals, and replacing his nutrition bag.

Ady has brought in loads of children's books. She reads them every night to the baby like Steel would be doing. One of the books catches my attention. On the cover, there is a boy sitting on his grandpa's lap, a fireplace burning and an old wooden clock standing in the corner.

It reminds me of Kell's pocket watch. I wanted so much to give it back to him, but the timing was never right. I reach in my bag and take it out. I mimic how Kell would rub his fingers on it and open it up. I know he'll never be a part of my life again. Since I can't have children, I've decided that this baby will one day know the story of Kell and will become the owner of his watch.

"When will Mrs. Nolan be back?"

I'm startled from my thoughts by the doctor's voice. "She should be here soon."

"Good, I want her here when we recover Steel today. I'm very hopeful, his numbers look good since we turned off his medication a couple hours ago." He smiles.

"Oh, my God! That's the best news!" I stand up and hug him. "I'll get ahold of my family so they can all be here."

I quickly get on my link with Syn. They are only five minutes out. I update him but ask him not to tell Ady until she gets here. I link with the rest of my family. They are all on their way.

Five minutes later, Ady waddles in the room. "Syn said you had some news for me." She looks hopeful.

"The doctor was just in here and he said that Steel has improved so much that they are going to try and wake him up," I say almost bouncing with joy.

Tears immediately fill her eyes and her knees buckle. Syn is able to catch her and lead her to the chair beside Steel. Her tears continue to fall. "I can't believe this day is finally here. I was starting to doubt that he'd ever wake up."

I see her wince and hold her belly. "Are you okay?" I ask as I dab her face with tissues to dry up her tears.

"I think the baby knows. It just kicked me really hard."

The doctor walks in and shakes hands with Syn before he squats in front of Ady. He explains to her the process of rewarming him and that it may take a few hours, but he feels that the outcome will be good. He walks over to the machine and presses a few buttons and the glass chamber that has enclosed Steel raises up. He disconnects some of the tubes.

"Can I touch him?" Ady tentatively asks.

"Absolutely." The doctor smiles.

She reaches out and touches him. She draws her hand back quickly as if she has been burned. "He's so cold!" she cries.

"He will warm up slowly," the doctor responds.

Within an hour, everyone has arrived. Ady takes the time to catch them up to speed on what the doctor has said. I notice that she has kept a hand on her lower belly the entire time. She walks back over to the bed and holds Steel's hand. She keeps one hand on her belly.

I walk over to her and whisper in her ear. "Are you sure you're okay?" I point to her baby bump.

"I'm more uncomfortable than usual and the baby is so active today. I think it's excited about its daddy." She smiles.

"Maybe you should let me walk you over to your doctor's office—so he can make sure everything is alright."

"I'm fine. I'm not leaving until I see the whites of his eyes," she says sternly.

"It may be a few hours. It won't take us that long to get you checked out."

"I'm fine," she assures me.

I'm not buying it. I will appease her, but I'm not taking my eyes off of her.

The waiting has everyone on edge and it has grown eerily quiet. "I can't just stand here anymore!" Syn barks as he lunges his frame up from off the wall where he was leaning, startling all of us.

"He moved! Ady yells. "He moved his fingers."

We all crowd around him and watch as he slowly tries to open his eyes.

"That's it, Steel. Come back to me!" Ady cries.

Before I can fully see the lavender of his eyes. His mouth parts open and breathes out Ady's name. She is leaning over him, hugging him to her. His arm slowly comes up and holds her back. The room is filled with happy tears. Ady finally releases him so that everyone else can see him. It takes a little while to get his bearings and a voice that is louder than a whisper.

"What happened to me?" His question is pointed at Syn.

"Do you remember anything?" Syn asks.

He blinks his eyes a few times. "The last thing I remember was that all of you were coming over for dinner so that we could tell you about Kell."

My heart aches at the mention of his name. Steel glances around the room as he sits up for the first time.

"Where is he?"

Everyone's eyes are on me. "A lot has happened in the past few months," is all I can say.

"Months?" Steel frowns.

Kyren steps up. "Why don't you ladies take a break? Let us catch Steel up on things."

Ady stands and Steel's eyes grow big at her much larger belly and his hand reaches out and touches her. "You're beautiful," he says.

"God, I have missed you!" She cries again and he kisses her belly.

The only dry pair of eyes in the room are mine. I can't let myself go there. "Ady, you haven't eaten all day. How about we go get you some food?"

Surprisingly she doesn't argue. She stops for a kiss from Steel and follows me out of the room. I take her hand to lead her to the cafeteria and she stops me.

"I think we need to go visit my doctor now," she says wincing.

I don't ask her any questions. We change direction and head to the OB floor.

I'm holding Ady's hand as the doctor tells her that she is 6 cm dilated. "It's a month too early."

"With all the stress you have been under, I'm surprised you made it this far. But the baby looks fine. A little small, but fine. Let's get you admitted."

"Wait! No, I need to be with Steel! Can't you stop the labor? I don't think he is strong enough to deal with this right now." She attempts to get off the table.

I place my hand on her shoulder. "Let me take care of things with him. I don't care how weak Steel is, he would not miss this for the world. How ironic do you think it is that he woke up on the day you're going to deliver his child?" I kiss her on the forehead and turn to the doctor. "Get her settled, while I go get her husband."

I walk into Steel's hospital room and he is sitting up taking sips of water. When his eyes lock with mine, I see the sadness behind them. Obviously, they have told him about Kell. I don't want him to be sad, not after everything that he has been through.

"Gray, I'm so..."

I don't let him finish. "Ady is in labor!" I blurt out.

Everyone starts talking at once. "She's okay. The doctor said that the baby will be small, but fine. I need to take you to her."

Steel turns to get out of bed but waivers when he tries to stand. His mom and dad sit him back down.

"Not so fast son, you're too weak to walk anywhere," his mother states. "I'll get a wheelchair."

"Do you guys think you could help me get dressed? I don't want to meet my new baby in a hospital gown."

Ady has kept a bag of his clothes nearby since the first day Steel got here. I walk over to the small closet. I pull out jeans and a t-shirt for him and hand them to his dad. "I'll go sit with Ady, while you boys make him presentable." Before I leave the room, I kiss Steel on the cheek. "I'm so glad you made it back to us."

He grabs my hand. By the look in his eyes, I know he wants to say something about Kell, but instead... "Thanks for taking such good care of Ady for me."

Pieces of Gray

"We all had a hand in that." I would never admit to him that Syn had to shake me up a bit to get me to focus on something other than myself.

We all impatiently wait inside the waiting room. It's been such a long day between waiting on Steel to wake up and now Ady to deliver the baby. I sit back and watch my family as they talk amongst themselves and I feel blessed. I love all of them. This is one strong family.

I have the ache of missing Kell, but I know that I am loved and can get through anything with the people in this room. Today was a miracle and for the first time in a long time, I'm happy and I know that I will be okay. A smile slips on my face and Syn catches it and winks at me.

A few moments later, a nurse is wheeling Steel out with a baby in his arms and he is all smiles. "It's a girl!" We all surround him to take a look at the newest member of our family.

"How is Ady?" I ask.

"She's doing okay. The doctor let her hold the baby for a bit and then gave her something to help her sleep."

"Do we have a name for this little princess?" Syn asks.

The proud papa smiles. "Lauren Esme Nolan."

I love that they used both the names that they liked. "She's beautiful."

"Good thing she looks like her mother," Syn ribs him.

"She is stunning. She gets her beauty from the women in this family. She has her grandmother's lavender eyes." Aunt Brogan takes her from Steel and kisses all over her.

CHAPTER

22

Life has finally gotten back to normal. Ady and Steel are home with their new baby, who is already sleeping through the night. Steel is getting physical therapy every day and is regaining his strength. Aunt Brogan, Uncle Kyren, and my parents all went back to Maine, but not before having their house plans drawn up to start building here in the next couple of months.

Syn went back to work. He has been kind of distant the last couple of weeks. I'm not sure what's going on with him. I'm sure it has to be odd not having Kell around. I know they'd become good friends and work partners. He doesn't mention him by name, but I think that has to do more with me than him. I'm meeting up with him today after one of my dog training sessions. Maybe I can get him to talk to me.

He's already seated at a table when I arrive. He's talking to someone in hushed tones on his portable computer link when I sit down. He tells whoever it is goodbye and closes the cover.

"I didn't mean to interrupt," I comment as he stands and pulls out my chair.

"I was just finishing up some business." He sits back down and pours me a glass of water from the carafe in the middle of the table.

I purposely keep our conversation light until our food arrives, hoping for no interruptions. "I've missed seeing you around." I start.

"I've been buried in work since..." He stops himself.

"It's okay, you can say his name. I promise I won't break." I touch his hand.

He clears his throat. "Since Kell left." He stares at me for a moment. "I've been working on a difficult case."

"I think it's more than that. You have been distant with all of us."

He sits back into his chair. "Something has been missing." He blows out.

"You mean more than just Kell?"

"I'm talking about my life. I watch my brother with his wife and family. I see how happy they are together. And when you and...Kell were together, you beamed happiness." He takes a sip of water. "I think maybe I've missed out on a chance at the same thing."

I'm totally floored. "I thought you were happy all these years playing the field?"

"Well, I haven't been unhappy." He smiles. "I've never met anyone that makes me want to stick around, and now, even if that is what I wanted, I don't know that I would meet someone who wanted to stick with me for any length of time."

I stop eating and put my fork down. "Why would you say that? You would be a great catch!" He chuckles and shakes his head no. "I'm serious. Look, I know you have a rough, tough exterior, but I know the heart of the man underneath it all. You love deeply with every part of your being. Any woman would be lucky to have your heart."

"Yeah, if she could just get past me being an asshole."

"You said she... Have you met someone?"

"I've met someone that is a pain in my ass." He laughs.

I sit back and smile at him.

195

"What are you grinning at?" His smile is gone.

"She will be the one."

He snorts. "Hell no, this one is as wild as they come."

"Kind of like you?" My voice goes up an octave.

"No, way. This one would have my balls if I even thought about getting into her pants." He laughs.

"Sounds like your kind of challenge to me."

"Then you don't know me very well. All I have ever had to do was lay on the charm and give them this smile," he says grinning like the Cheshire cat.

"Maybe it's time for something different." My smile fades because I know what's coming next.

"Does that go for you, too?" He places his elbows on the table and his chin perched on his hands.

"I'm doing okay on my own. When I'm ready, I'll move on. I'm not saying it will be easy and I don't know that I will ever love someone as much as I loved Kell and that scares me. Wherever he is, I hope that he's happy. I honestly want him to have a good life. Obviously, I was not meant to be part of his anymore. I'm ready to let go."

"How pray tell are you going to do that?"

"I'm taking a little trip to somewhere that I have nothing but good memories of him and I'm going to tell him goodbye in my own way."

"Nothing dangerous, I hope?" He lifts his eyebrows.

"Nope, I'm done with anything dangerous anymore. I want to be around to watch my niece grow into a beautiful, badass woman like her Auntie." I laugh.

"If she's anything like the women in this family, then I have no doubt she will be a badass."

His computer link chirps. As he lifts the cover, I see a smile I have never seen on him before. It's the look of a man in love. I'd never say that to him, because all he would do is deny it.

"I really need to answer this link. Thanks for meeting me for lunch." He starts to get up. "And Gray..." He kisses the top of my head. "Have a good trip."

Cy and I are all packed and ready to go. I want to check in on Steel, Ady, and the baby before I take off for two weeks.

"Oh my God! I think she has grown just since yesterday," I say as I pick up Lauren. She gives me a wide toothless grin. "I can't believe she's already three months old."

"I know. Steel is already asking when we are having another one." She elbows him in the ribs.

"Good Lord! Give the woman a break! She's been through enough this year." I laugh.

"Can't blame a man for trying. Besides, I like the practice." He hugs Ady to his side and she blushes.

"Well, I can see things are back to normal around here." I laugh again and kiss the baby. "She does have the most beautiful eyes."

"I know my mom and I have always hated the color of our eyes. But on her, they're simply beautiful."

"Three months old and she already has you wrapped around her little finger." I shake my head and smile.

He sits down in the pink cushioned rocking chair. "I just wish after three months that I was back to normal."

"You look good, Steel. You move a little slower, but you look good. Give it some more time."

"He works out like a maniac. Then, he wonders why he's so exhausted," Ady adds.

"I just want to be back to normal strength."

"And the doctor said you will be, but you need to give it more time." She kisses him sweetly.

I hand Lauren back to Ady. "I'm leaving you two lovebirds alone."

"Do have everything you need?" Steel asks.

"Yes, here's the address of where I will be staying."

Steel unfolds the piece of paper. "Isn't this..."

"Yes. It is," I answer before he has time to grill me on it. "I love you all. I'll be back in a couple of weeks. And you little miss, don't grow anymore while I'm away."

The Pacific Coast is beautiful this time of year. The water is still chilly, but the air smells so fresh and crisp after a cold winter. There is just enough breeze to provide coolness to the air. I park and let Cy out, watching him as he runs to the ocean and jumps in the waves. This place is just as I remember it.

Peaceful.

I call Cy out of the ocean and he obediently follows me over the rickety bridge to the tree house. As soon as I step inside, I'm overtaken with vivid memories of Kell. I deliberately walk around the tree house and touch every place that we made love.

I thought this would be a good idea, but now that I'm here, I feel that familiar ache for him again. Somehow, I thought it would be easier to say goodbye to him in the last place I felt so connected to him. It made complete sense in my head, but my heart tells me another story.

I unpack my clothes and settle in. I decide to put my big girl panties on and do what I came here to do. I suck it up with a glass of wine and decide to enjoy the evening air. There is a perfectly comfy chair sitting out on the tiny porch that has my name written all over it. I set my bottle and glass of wine down and ease myself into the chair. I remember this chair well. Kell had me in an odd position bent over it, while he fucked me from behind. I rub the arm of the chair as if easing its pain. I remember it squeaking in protest.

Gah, I need another glass of wine. I fill it to the brim not once, but three more times. The last thing I remember is Cy curled at my feet, and me stroking his fur, telling him what a good dog he is.

Pieces of Gray

The sun is bright out already as I try to stretch out the sleepiness. I pull the blanket up over me for some warmth. Funny, I don't remember getting up and getting a blanket. I look at the bottle of wine and it is completely dry. No wonder I don't remember...I laugh to myself. I unfold from the chair and get up to make some coffee. While it's brewing, I change into some sweats. I haven't run in awhile and one of my goals is to start taking care of myself again. Besides, running is cathartic for me.

It takes me a minute to realize Cy isn't in the tree house. I call his name, but he doesn't come running like he usually does.

"Cy!" I yell again, as I step back out onto the porch. I listen for him, but the wind is blowing hard through the trees and I can't hear anything. It's not like him to leave my side. I rush back in and put my shoes on.

"Cy!" I keep yelling as I make it down to the beach. Off in the distance, I see him. Someone is throwing a ball in the water for him. I take off in a jog in his direction. As I get closer, he finally sees me and starts running toward me.

"There you are. You scared me," I scold, as he licks my face. The person he was playing with is walking my direction. I figure, whoever he is, he can't be a threat or Cy would be all over him. He's tall and has a gray hoodie on, he's not close enough yet for me to tell what he looks like.

He walks a little closer and stops. Cy runs back over to him and sits down beside him. I walk a little closer, and the man pulls off his hoodie.

I let out an audible gasp that can be heard over the wind. Standing in front of me is Kell. I'm frozen in place. I can't be in the same place as him. It's not possible.

I feel the burn of the air being drawn into my lungs. "Cy, come here." He immediately obeys and I grab him by the collar.

I can do this. I can step away from him. It takes everything in me to turn and take one step.

"Hi." I hear him say.

Take another step, I tell myself. My feet feel weighted down by the sand.

"Wait!" he yells this time.

Don't listen to him. Focus on the third step. My stride has shortened.

"I'm sorry." His words sound broken.

Come on fourth step—I can do this. My heart is breaking.

"Gray," he whispers it, but somehow I still hear it.

I slowly turn to face him. "How do you know my name?"

He steps up so close, that I can feel him on my skin. "I'm sorry that I couldn't help you with Steel when you needed me to," he says softly.

I take a faltering step back. "You remember?"

"I remember everything." He smiles and for a brief moment, I'm filled with hope and excitement.

I reach out to touch his arm. Maybe I'm still dreaming. When my hand touches his skin, I pull back quickly. He's real.

I take another step back. "But how?"

"I couldn't let them do it. I couldn't let them erase my memories of you again."

My moment of happiness turns into rage. "That was months ago and you show up now!" I yell and take off running to the tree house. I don't stop running until I make it inside. I turn to shut the door and he is right behind me. "Get the fuck out of here!" I yell at him.

"Please, hear me out," he pleads.

I slap him hard. I'm startled by it. I have never slapped anyone.

He doesn't even flinch. Instead, he steps closer to me. "I deserve that, but you will listen to what I have to say."

I want to throw something at him. I look around the room and I see the blanket laying on the bed. I pick it up and shove it at him."You did this. You were here last night and watched me sleep!"

"Yes. You were passed out in the chair when I got here. I didn't want to wake you up from your wine coma." He points to the empty bottle I placed on the counter. "You were cold, so I covered you up."

I'm so angry at this beautiful man standing in front of me. I try twice to speak. Nothing comes out but noise. He has the audacity to laugh at me.

I walk away from him and sit on the chair that I passed out in. He lets me stew for a minute before he takes his large frame and leans it on the railing in front of me. His legs are stretched out and crossed at the ankles. The palms of his hands are resting on the ledge behind him.

"Are you ready to hear what I have to say?" he grits out.

"Do I have a choice?" I snap

He looks hurt at my words. I immediately regret saying them. He uncrosses his legs and kneels in front of me. "Yes, you have a choice, but I'm really hoping you will give me a chance to explain."

I search his dark eyes that I know so well, all I see is love. I soften and all anger is gone. "I will listen."

"Right before the procedure to erase my memory, visions of you flashed through my head. Every moment we spent together, from the first time you stepped into my tent to the last time I touched you. It was all there." He swallows hard and I bite my lip to keep from crying.

"I remember every emotion, from a deep love to my greatest fear, the day you were on the roof giving yourself up to protect me.

I almost wanted to kill you myself for giving yourself up to save me, but I understood why you did it. I had never been so terrified in my life. I was more frightened then than I was when you told me you were a virgin."

A little laughter escapes me. "Why would that scare you?"

"Because, I knew how badly I wanted you and I was afraid of hurting you. That I would scare you so much that you would leave me." Tears are starting to well up behind his eyes.

I reach out and touch his face. "I never knew that. You seemed like you were so sure of yourself."

"That's what I wanted you to feel. I wanted you to feel safe and loved in my arms." He stands up and pulls me with him.

"I couldn't lose you again, so I told them to stop the procedure. I told them not to tell you anything. I wanted time to try and get my head together and if I couldn't you would have been none the wiser and you would eventually move on."

"Where have you been all this time?"

"In a lot of therapy. I also took a trip."

"Like a vacation?" I frown up at him, trying to understand.

He walks back over to the railing and he looks toward the water and leans on his forearms. I stand beside him, facing the treehouse.

"I went back to China."

"What? Please tell me you didn't... It's still not safe over there."

"I went in with a military unit. I had to go back to face my fears."

"But I already blew up the cave."

He chuckles. "I figured that was your handy work. We dug through the rubble and I made it back inside the cage."

"Why? Why would you do that?"I turn him around so that I can see his face.

"Because of you. I wanted to face my demons head on so that I could be free of them. So that I could be the man you fell in love with and not some ghost of him."

"Why would you risk your life like that?"

He grabs me to him and kisses me deeply, like a starving man. I'm completely breathless when he pulls away.

"How many times did you risk yourself for me? Your first risk was loving me and letting me steal your virginity. The second was the day you were on that roof. The third is when you didn't tell me you lost our baby because God knows I'd have gotten us all killed.

Fourth, is when you when you chose to let me go. Fifth, is when you let me back in, knowing damn good and well what the consequences could be. Do I need to go on?"

Our eyes are locked. "I did all those things because I loved you. Well...except for the virginity part. I did that for purely selfish reasons." This time I kiss him breathless. He walks me backward to the chair. I stop when I feel it behind me.

"Are you okay now?" I need to know.

"I'm better, some days are a struggle, that's why I waited to come and find you. I wanted to be sure that I could be the man you deserve. That you'd never lose me again." He consumes my mouth. His hands find their way under my shirt and he lets out a moan.

"That has to be the sexiest sound I've ever heard." It ignites me and I can't wait to have my hands on him. We are ripping each other's clothes off until we are down to nothing but bare skin.

We both take a step back and soak each other in. He looks a little leaner than the last time I saw him. I let my eyes travel down his chiseled abs. I love the sexy V at his waist and his beautiful cock that stands at attention. It's thick and full and has a vein that runs downward and to the left.

It pulsates as I lick my lips. I hear a groan and then I'm pushed into the chair.

"Don't even think about putting those beautiful lips on my cock. I wouldn't last a minute," he says. He leans down and begins to achingly suck in one of my nipples. I feel my body start to throb again.

I reach down and pull his hair so that he will look at me. He grabs my hands and holds them on the arms of the chair.

"I'm going to devour every inch of your gorgeous body before I let you put your hands on me," he growls and continues his glorious torture. His hands and mouth have not even left my breasts before my first orgasm hits me. He chuckles as I ride the wave of pleasure.

"That's one," he says.

"We're counting? If that's the case, then we are going one for one mister."

"God, I hope so," he growls.

He continues his downward path until he has me spread wide for him. He plunges his mouth down on me. I have missed his tongue. He makes circles and then sucks. I'm on the edge of another orgasm when he sticks his fingers inside me. I clench around them bucking my hips off the chair.

"That's two," he says as he spreads my legs over the arms of the chair. I want to touch him so badly. I quickly lean forward and grab his growing cock. I start to stroke him before he can stop me.

"Fuck, baby!" He groans and I watch him as he explodes in my hands. I love that he lost control.

"One," I say, mocking him.

He picks me up and bends me over the back of the chair. He gives me a quick swat on the ass and I yelp. He rubs me where his hand smacked me. His other hand is in the center of my back holding me down.

He leans into me and I feel him grow hard again. He bites my ear, "I'm not anywhere near done with you."

I fight to get up because I want my hands on him again, but he grabs my hips and pulls them backward and roughly enters me. I gasp at the sensation of him entering me from behind. My hands are ripping at the cloth of the chair.

One of his hands snakes around and pulls at my nipple, while the other one finds its way between my legs. I release my grip and reach down and place my hand on top of his and then reach a little further. I want to feel where we are joined together.

I hear him hiss through his teeth and I know he's about to lose control again. The sound of him fighting it brings me to another spiral. I feel my body throb around him. "Kell!" I scream his name into the wind.

As soon as his name leaves my lips, he lets out a roar and pumps into me so hard that I have to steady myself by leaning further over the chair and holding on tightly. He rides out his orgasm, as his fingers claw into my hips marking his territory.

"God, I've missed you," he hisses as he turns me back around to face him. He kisses me sweetly. "I wanted to go all day with you, but you're killing me."

"I lost count, but I think I still owe you." I laugh at him

"You have to give me a little bit of time, then I'll let you make it up to me." He nips my nose.

We lay in bed for the next hour talking and touching one another. This is no ghost of the man I remember. He is the only man I've ever loved. I hop out of bed and grab my bag.

"What are you doing? Get back in bed." He pulls the covers back, and I can see that he is hard again.

"I've wanted to give this back to you for a long time." I hand him his family heirloom.

"You kept this? How did you keep...?" He chokes on his words.

"I stashed it on the roof before they came up to get me. When I was rescued, I thought you were dead. I was frantic to get my hands on it, so I still had a piece of you with me. I went back to the rooftop. It was still there. A little weathered, but I could still carry it with me

I took it to a horologist and had it restored. There aren't too many people that work on antique watches anymore, I was lucky to find someone local. The guy thought it was a little weird that I wouldn't let him fix the time on it."

As I crawl back into bed with him, he opens the cover of the watch and moves the hands. "What are you doing?"

"I want it set to the time my heart started beating again. The exact moment I saw you on the beach today."

That's the final straw for holding back my tears. The floodgates open and I sob into his chest. He just lets me cry as he strokes my hair. "I love you, baby. I will never let you go again." When I'm all cried out, he makes love to me again. Taking his time, being so sweet and gentle that I never wanted it to end.

We spent the next two weeks thoroughly enjoying each other. I felt a little tinge of guilt that I didn't let my family know that Kell was back, but I was completely selfish wanting him all to myself.

CHAPTER

"**W**hy are you so quiet?" I ask him. He has nervously been biting his lower lip the entire ride home. "Are you worried about seeing my family?"

"No, not at all. I love your family."

I put the Jeep in park as we make it to my house. Cy jumps out and takes off after Steel's dogs. "What is it then?"

"I haven't um… been completely honest with you?" He says and bites his lip again.

I'm a little afraid of what he might tell me. "What haven't you been honest about?"

"I knew where to find you because I came here first. Steel told me where you were."

"Wait, so all that time I spent catching you up on what happened to Steel and Ady having the baby you already knew?" I frown. "Why didn't you just tell me?"

"Well, I like listening to you talk and I wanted to hear how you really handled all of it. And…"

There he goes biting his lip again. "And… what?"

"I wanted to spend the time alone with you because I have a surprise for you."

I climb out of the Jeep. "You know good and well that I don't like surprises."

He climbs out and meets me at the back of the Jeep, grabbing our bags. "I know, but I hope like hell you like this one." He takes my hand and starts walking toward Steel's house.

"Why aren't we going to my house?"

"Because the surprise is at Steel's."

We walk in and I hear Syn counting to ten. "Ready or not here I come," he warns.

"Okay, now I know Syn has lost his mind. Lauren is a little too young for hide and seek," I whisper to Kell. Then I hear laughter coming from behind the couch. Syn ducks behind it, and I hear a little girl squeal.

Before I can investigate, Steel, Ady, and the baby come into the room with an older woman that I've never seen before. All of them stop in their tracks and stare at me like I have three heads.

"What?" I ask and Syn's head pops up from behind the couch.

"Oh…hey," he says as he stands up.

"Did I miss something?" I ask.

A little curly headed girl peeks over the couch. "Daddy!" she yells and runs into Kell's arms.

I take a step back from him and everyone continues to stare at me. "This is your surprise? You have a daughter?" I stammer.

He picks her up and kisses her cheek and then turns her toward me. "Yes…I mean, WE have a daughter."

I'm completely dumbfounded. "I think I would remember if we had a daughter…" I say a little too harshly. All I can think about is that he had a child with another woman and never told me. How is that even possible? The little girl only looks to be about three years old.

The older woman steps up and takes the little girl from him. "Let me take your baby, Mr. Crew, while you talk to her." She smiles sweetly at me.

Ady finally speaks to me. "Please, come sit down. We can explain."

"We? What do you guys have to do with all of this?" I sit while I'm talking.

"They helped take care of her so that I could go to you."

"Why would you put that on Steel and Ady? You know what they've been through. They have their hands full with their own baby."

"It was no bother. He hired a nanny. It's been awesome!" Ady gushes beaming.

"I still don't understand," I huff.

Kell gets on his knees in front of me. Syn sits beside me. "Remember when I told you that I went to China?"

"Yes, to heal."

"While I was at the military base, one of the units found a little girl out in the jungle. Her parents had been killed and she was wandering around her house for days, barefoot and hungry before she was found. She has no other family. They were just going to send her to an orphanage back in the states. Her mom and dad were originally from Iowa. They were on a teaching mission and were killed in their home while they slept."

He holds my hand. "The moment I laid eyes on her I fell in love with her," he swallows hard, "she would be about the same age as our child would have been."

I've heard his words but my mind is swimming. "You adopted her?"

"Yes." His eyes are pleading for something.

I think I'm in shock. Yes. That's it, shock. He miraculously shows back up in my life and I couldn't be happier about it. Now he tells me "we,"... he said "we" have a child, too.

A DAUGHTER.

A THREE-year-old daughter.

A beautiful, curly haired, brown-eyed little girl, who just called Kell daddy.

"Gray, are you okay? Did you hear me?" he asks.

I look at him. Then I look at Syn. My eyes keep jumping back and forth.

"You okay, sweetheart?" Syn puts his arm around me.

"You were playing with her," I accuse quietly.

"Yeah, well she's a cute little thing. She already loves her Uncle Syn."

Ady and Steel step into view. "She's so sweet, and she just loves Lauren. She can't quit kissing her cheeks," Ady says.

"What if she doesn't like me?" I whisper my fears.

"Oh, baby! She is going to love you." Kell smiles. "I promise."

"I don't know." I breathe out. It took me a while to come to terms with the fact that I would never have children. This is all so overwhelming." I get up. "I need a minute."

Kell starts to say something, but Syn stops him with a wave of his hand. I push my way through everyone gathered in the living room. I storm outside for some much needed fresh air.

I make my way to the ledge and look out over the water. I hear the dogs barking in the distance and see the Nanny and the little curly haired girl playing ball with them. I watch them and did not realized that my feet were moving toward them.

What am I so afraid of? I love children. Maybe it's not her that scares me. Maybe it's because I've lost Kell three times. I love him with everything in me. But honestly, how do I know he's really okay and ready for all of this?

"You're over-thinking it." Kell's arms wrap around me.

"How do you know what I'm thinking?" I reach behind and place my hand on his cheek.

"Your doubts aren't about her. They're about us."

I turn in his arms. "You're only partially right. I have no doubt about my part in this relationship."

"Ouch," he says.

"Let me finish. I've lost you three times. What if in a few months you can't handle any of this and you need out?"

"I can promise you that no matter what happens, I will never leave you. I have made tremendous progress in the months that I was gone. I did that for us. I don't want a life without you in it. You are my world. This little girl is now a part of it."

We stand there in silence for a long moment and hold each other. I feel little arms wrap around my legs.

"I hug Daddy, too."

Kell bends down and picks her up. I run my hands through her thick locks.

"Sweetie, I want you to meet your new mommy," Kell says kissing the top of her head.

"Hi, Mommy," she says with the sweetest voice.

"Hi..." I realize I don't even know her name. "What's your name, sweetie?" Well, that was certainly awkward. I hope years from now, she won't need therapy from Mommy not knowing her child's name.

"My name's Bronte." She grins at me.

I smile up at Kell. "You are kidding me. You actually changed her name to Bronte?"

"No, I swear that's her real name. It was fate that she be ours."

Kismet. Karma. Serendipity.

I kiss her little nose. "What a beautiful name for a beautiful little girl."

By bedtime, I'm madly in love with Bronte. She feels like she belongs to us already. I built a pallet on the floor for her next to our bed and she's fast asleep. I snuggle in bed next to Kell.

"She's so beautiful. Thank you for bringing her home."

"She felt like home to me the minute I saw her." He kisses me gently.

"You know our home isn't big enough now..." I say strumming my fingers on his bare chest.

"I like that you said our home. Steel and I have already come up with a plan to add on." He kisses me again.

"I spoke with my mom. She can't wait to meet her new granddaughter."

"I think their house here might get built a little faster than what they planned," he says between kisses.

"I've never been as happy as I am right at this moment."

"My life mission is to make the two woman in my life happy every day." He sits up abruptly. "I have one more surprise for you." He reaches into his bag that's by the bed.

"Please, no more surprises! Get back under the covers with me." Actually, I'm slowly warming to the idea of surprises. I won't tell him that, in case he goes overboard.

He sits Indian style facing me. "I love you, Gray Milby, with all my heart. Will you make me the happiest man alive and marry me for real this time?"

He opens a black velvet box. My hands are shaking as I take it. It's a silver ring with a huge square diamond standing in the middle. "Oh my God! It's beautiful!" I put it in my lap and start hugging and kissing him all over his face.

"Is that a yes, then?" he asks laughing. "Or at least, a maybe?"

"Yes, yes, yes!" I chant as I place my hands on either side of his face and kiss him deeply.

He pulls back and grabs the box and takes out the ring. I hold my hand up for him and he places it on my finger. "Let's do this." He smiles. I pull him under the covers.

ACKNOWLEDGEMENTS

First and Foremost, thank you to all the readers, reviewers, bloggers, my street team and all my Newsletter fans. Without all of your support I couldn't continue to do what I love – write. Your support amazes me.

To Kennedy Kelly – Thank you for the countless hours you put into making my cover, teasers, and trailer. You do beautiful and professional work.

To Tami Rogers – Thank you for your countless hours of editing my book and trying to keep me straight.

To Keshia Bowling my Beta Reader -Thank you for reading all of my books and keeping me on track. More importantly, thank you for your friendship.

To Monica Corwin – Thanks for all your help in making my books look beautiful on the inside.

To Peyton Meachum my beautiful niece – Thank you for letting me use your picture on the cover. You are a beautiful model.

To Mandi Nelson – Thank you for always helping me with my cover ideas.

To Roy Moore – without you, none of this would be possible.

ABOUT THE AUTHOR

Kelly Moore was raised in Mt. Dora, Florida, a true southern girl with a sarcastic wit. Gypsy traveling nurse by day and romantic author by night. Loves all things romantic with a little spice and humor. Loves two characters who over comes their pasts to fall in love and have a happy ending. Wife, mother, grandmother and dog lover. Travels the US in a fifth wheel making memories and making friends.

www.kellymooreauthor.com

Made in the USA
Middletown, DE
11 August 2022

71092750R00132